No One Sees Me 'Til I Fall

Also by Jen J. Danna and Ann Vanderlaan

<u>Abbott and Lowell Forensic Mysteries</u>

Dead, Without a Stone to Tell It
No One Sees Me 'Til I Fall
A Flame in the Wind of Death
Two Parts Bloody Murder
Lament the Commons Bones

<u>FBI K-9s</u>
(Writing as Sara Driscoll)

Lone Wolf
Before It's Too Late
Storm Rising
No Man's Land (coming December 2019)

Kindle™ editions available through Amazon.
Also available in Kobo™/Nook™ e-book formats.

No One Sees Me 'Til I Fall

Abbott and Lowell Forensic Mysteries

Jen J. Danna

with Ann Vanderlaan

ISBN: 978-1-7751578-6-1

First Edition: July 2019

Printed by Kindle Direct Publishing™, An Amazon.com Company.

Cover design by Jess Danna
Copyright© 2013, 2019 Jess Danna Photography and Jen J. Danna
jessdanna.com
Cover model: Jordan Newton

AUTHOR'S NOTE

The title of this novella comes from the poem "Until I Fall" by HaliJo Webster Oickle (used with permission).

I shout and no one seems to hear.

I dance naked and no one responds.

I wow my "self" and stand higher

than any mountain I have stood on before!

No one sees me.

Not till I fall.

ACKNOWLEDGMENTS

Many thanks to the Newton clan for all their work behind the scenes on this novella. To my husband Rick, who once again shouldered formatting the print version, and to my daughters Jess and Jordan for joining forces to produce the cover—Jordan who was a good sport in appearing as the cover model, and Jess, the photographer and graphic designer behind the cover. I couldn't have done it without you all!

J.J.D.

PROLOGUE: BOKEH

Bokeh: an Anglicized version of the Japanese noun *boke* 暈け, which means blur or haze. Bokeh is a subjective measure of the aesthetic quality of areas in an image that are "out of focus". It is especially important in portraiture where areas behind the subject should be as smooth and non-distracting as possible.

Tuesday, 3:03 a.m.
Lawrence Municipal Landfill
Lawrence, Massachusetts

Death had not come gently. No thief stealing silently in the night, but rather a brutal force, taking life and hope with it. Leaving behind only the nameless. The faceless.

Inside the security fence, the bag fell to the ground with a heavy *thud*, and then a dark figure landed lightly beside it. He froze when the long wail of a siren sliced through the air, a scream in the night that set his heart pounding before the sound faded off into the distance.

They weren't coming for him.

Heaving the bag carelessly over his shoulder, he bent low and loped awkwardly over the open ground toward the dark mass. The stench was nearly overwhelming, but he pushed forward, climbing the slippery slope nearly to the top. He let the bag slide from his back to topple onto the pile, already blending into the trash surrounding it.

A sliver of moon slipped out from behind the clouds, its light glinting over the smooth plastic surface. But it could not touch what was inside. Locked in the dark forever.

The man turned and skidded down the incline before retracing his steps and scrambling over the fence once again.

He didn't turn around to look back at what he had done.

It was already forgotten.

CHAPTER ONE: EXPOSURE

Exposure: a measure of the amount of light hitting the surface of a light-sensitive photographic material while creating a latent image.

Friday, 1:37 p.m.
Boston University, School of Medicine
Boston, Massachusetts

Massachusetts State Police Trooper Leigh Abbott hesitated at the open door to the laboratory. Her gaze instantly found her onetime partner—Boston University forensic anthropologist Dr. Matthew Lowell—huddled with his graduate students around an examination table across the room. Tall and dark, his physique spoke of long hours spent at the oars out on the Charles River, and he stood a full head above his students, except long, lanky Paul Layne. The discussion was too quiet for Leigh to hear distinct words, but there was a thread of remorse in Kiko's tone, followed by cool logic in Matt's. Between Juka and Paul, she caught a glimpse of smooth ivory bones on the stainless steel table. The group was hard at work, examining human remains recovered from the charnel house beneath Boston's historic Old North Church.

Guilt coiled with anticipation in her gut. It had only been a few weeks since she'd first interrupted their work to pull them into a case. And yet here she was, proverbial hat in hand, once again.

She tapped two knuckles against the door frame.

Matt looked up from beneath the slightly shaggy hair that tended to fall into his eyes—a tactic she knew he employed to hide the twisted scar that ran from near his right eyebrow into his hairline. His expression warmed as their eyes met. "Trooper." He raised two fingers to his temple in a brief salute, the formality of the gesture tempered by a wide grin. "This is a surprise."

"Can't I just drop by the lab?" As Leigh approached the group, Kiko Niigata, Matt's senior grad student, stepped aside, making a place for her at the table. The group closed ranks around her, bringing her naturally into their circle. "What are you working on?"

"More remains from the charnel house," Kiko, a slender woman with delicate Japanese features, pointed to the tiny, anatomically-arranged skeleton, topped by a blossom of skull fragments.

"It's a newborn baby who probably died during childbirth, possibly along with its mother." Juka Petrović, stocky and solid, with the dark coloring of his Bosnian ancestors, gave her a short nod of greeting and a small smile. Always restrained, Juka's acknowledgement was the equivalent of the exuberant Paul greeting her with a trumpet fanfare.

"What happened to the skull?" In her peripheral vision, Leigh could see Paul's expression of cocky expectation, his gaze fixed on her face as if trying to read her mind. *He knows something's up.*

Matt picked up a tiny, gently curving piece of bone rimmed by ragged edges. "Nothing sinister. The fetal skull is actually comprised of forty-four unfused pieces. It's the flexibility of the unfused skull that allows passage through the birth canal. Later in life, the progression of skull fusion helps us determine age." He set the bone back into place in the human jigsaw puzzle. "Kiko's going to do the skull reconstruction, and then try to give our baby a face."

Kiko stroked an index finger over the curve of a tiny eye socket. "It's going to be a tough reconstruction because of all the suture lines, but Matt's willing to let me try."

Matt patted her shoulder. "It always bothers you to work with kids."

"And babies are the worst." She frowned down at the table. "So many died so young back then."

"Enough with the small talk," Paul finally exploded, drawing everyone's eyes. "You have a case for us, don't you?"

Leigh's gaze shot to Matt as confusion and then suspicion streaked across his face. She closed her eyes, guilt suddenly weighing heavily across her shoulders. She'd known there was a good chance Matt would misconstrue her arrival, especially considering the very private dinner they'd enjoyed last week—a dark restaurant, a good meal, fine wine, and a warm goodbye to end the evening. An evening his students and her sergeant were totally unaware of. "Well, now that you mention it . . ." she said weakly.

Matt stepped back from the exam table, his eyes narrowed as he considered her. "I should have seen it."

"Seen what?"

"You." One extended hand panned down, then back up her body. "This isn't a social call. You're in cop mode—hair tied back, plain business suit, sensible shoes, no jewelry." He crossed his arms over his broad chest and Leigh felt the space between them grow wider even though neither had moved. "I guess I called it right after all. What have you got for us, Trooper?"

Guilt started to dissipate as irritation rose. She knew how well they worked together . . . once they struggled to get on the same page. "Now don't go getting all out of sorts before I've even had a chance to bring you up to speed."

"I knew it!" Paul fist-pumped the air. "We're back, baby!"

"You really have a case for us?" Kiko asked. "Seriously?"

"Seriously. Interested?"

"Damn straight." Paul did a quick-footed hip-hop shuffle. "We're back to crime fighting. Cool!"

Leigh turned to Juka to find his gaze fixed on Matt, as if trying to temper his own response based on his supervisor's. "Juka? Are you willing to help out?"

The young man shifted uncertainly from foot to foot. "I'd be interested in another case. But only if Matt is. This should be his decision."

"I agree," Kiko said. "I'm happy to get involved again, and I know we were a valuable part of the last investigation. But this has to be Matt's call. He's the one who'll end up in court as the expert witness at the end of the case, not us."

Taking a deep breath, Leigh faced Matt. His hazel eyes were fixed unblinkingly on hers and his face was carefully blank. "So . . .

can I give you a rundown on my new case?" she asked cheerfully. She tried to match her words with an enticing smile, but it slipped when he continued to silently stare. "Matt?"

Instead of answering, he took her arm, drawing her toward his desk and out of earshot of his students. "You had this planned all along didn't you? You were going to use my students as leverage to get me on board. You knew they'd be interested, especially Paul. And you banked on their enthusiasm to drag me in whether I wanted to or not." He turned his back to the young people across the room, the only privacy afforded in the big, open lab. "Couldn't you have trusted me with the truth? I don't like games, Leigh. After all we've been through, I expect better from you than this."

Her head bowed, she rubbed a hand over the back of her neck, trying to ease some of the prickly stress suddenly lodged there. "I'm not playing games. I just really need your help. And I felt desperate enough to try to force your hand." She looked up when his hand closed over hers, pulling it from her neck to hold it in his, his thumb softly stroking over her skin.

"Then just ask me."

His gentle tone had her blinking up at him in surprise. "Really?"

"Really."

"Even after the last time?" Their successful first case together had brought them very much to the attention of the media and her superiors. But this wasn't the essence of her question—there were personal elements in play here they were both aware of, even if they seldom spoke of them.

Her gaze flicked up over his dark hair where a new scar joined the others cruelly carved into his flesh. "You got shot, hit on the head, and then we were both nearly killed by a maniac. And all those victims. Not to mention I practically blackmailed you into coming on board in the first place by threatening to take the case to a rival anthropologist."

"You didn't blackmail me."

She grimaced. "Actually, I did. I knew walking into the Old North that you didn't like Trevor Sharpe, so he was my last ditch ace-in-the-hole if you wouldn't sign on voluntarily." She tried to tug her hand from his, surprised when he didn't let go in disgust, and then shocked when he gave a short bark of laughter. "You're not mad?"

"How can I be mad when it got us here? Even I have to admit you were very resourceful. You knew what you wanted and went after it using any and all means at your disposal." He gave her hand a quick squeeze and then surreptitiously dropped it. "But next time, why don't you just pick up the phone. By this point we can cut right to the chase. Now, how about you fill us in?"

They rejoined the group, the three students watching them warily until Matt said, "Leigh's going to tell us what she knows. Then I assume we need to get out to a site right away? They're holding it for us?"

"Yes." She loosed a long sigh, her first relaxed breath since setting eyes on her victim. She pulled her notepad from her blazer pocket, flipping it open to the relevant details. "A call came in over the tip line yesterday reporting a body dumped in Lawrence's municipal landfill."

"A call? From who?" Matt asked.

"People don't usually leave their name on the tip line. Anonymity is the whole point. But it sounded like a girl."

"How do you find a body in a landfill?" Juka asked. "That must be a huge endeavor."

"Clearly they've found it or Leigh wouldn't be here," Matt interjected. "I'm betting they used a cadaver dog."

"Got it in one. They searched all yesterday afternoon without one with no luck. So this morning they brought in two dogs. One found the body stuffed in a garbage bag near the surface."

"I bet it blended right in like that." Paul pushed a hand through his dark blond hair, making it stand up in small spikes. "Without the phone tip, it might never have been found."

"It was clearly a recent addition, but would have been completely buried in another day or two. I was called in and I only needed one look to know that I needed you guys."

"There's no way the body's in good shape," Matt said. "Was the bag sealed?"

"It was until the local cops cut the bag open to confirm they had a victim."

Matt winced. "We need to move fast then. Birds and bugs infest dump sites in a big way."

"I left several officers with the remains, keeping the birds away."

"Bugs are the bigger contaminant at this point." Matt quickly moved through the lab, pulling equipment off shelves and out of drawers. "Get your field kits. Full Tyvek and sampling supplies." He glanced at Leigh. "I'll throw in coveralls for you too. You can't go rooting through garbage dressed like that." He paused for a moment, tapping an index finger against the benchtop. "I suspect a body bag might not do it for this one. Paul, you know that really big plastic transport container?"

"The one stored down the hall?"

"That's the one. Get it. We'll need it to hold the body bag." He turned back to Leigh. "Call in a morgue van. If we transport the body in my SUV, I'll never get the smell out."

"They're already on alert and waiting for my call. And you're right. I don't think a body bag will do it."

Matt stopped short, glancing back over his shoulder at her. "How bad is it?"

Leigh had spent the last hour trying to forget what she'd seen inside that plastic bag. "I'd use the word 'soup' but then I might never eat lunch again."

Matt nodded as if this was what he expected, and continued gathering his things and stuffing them into a backpack. "The body won't necessarily have been there long. Heat produced by landfill sites combined with warm weather and possible direct sunlight would turn the bag into an oven, speeding up decomp. It's going to be a putrefied mess. But that will probably save us maceration time."

Guilt and some of the stress lifted from Leigh's shoulders as she watched Matt and his students efficiently move around the lab, getting ready to start a new case.

Together they'd stopped a killer who'd flown below the radar for years, until she'd joined forces with Matt and his team. After the case ended, she thought their work together was done. But it looked like she was wrong.

The team was back.

CHAPTER TWO: EMULSION

Emulsion: the light-sensitive layer coating photographic film or paper. A latent image is formed in the emulsion when photographic film or paper is exposed to light.

Friday, 3:22 p.m.
Lawrence Municipal Landfill
Lawrence, Massachusetts

Leigh adjusted her tentative balance on the mound of trash, loose items shifting precariously under her booted feet. The effort not to breathe left her feeling light-headed, but every lungful of air was like inhaling fire, and her eyes stung from the fumes rising above the pile. To her right, a massive bulldozer climbed the steep incline, pushing more trash into place. Disturbed by the huge machine, a large flock of seagulls gave a collective angry squawk, and rose into the air in a cloud of flapping wings.

Leigh scanned her surroundings: Around her was practically every item she could ever imagine passing through human hands—plastic and glass bottles, paper products, Styrofoam cups, torn clothing, soiled diapers, rotting food, and furniture. All carelessly discarded.

Just like the victim at her feet.

Staring down at the tangle of putrefied flesh, Leigh couldn't help the shiver of pity running down her spine, leaving her cold despite the brilliant autumn sunshine. A life not only cut short, but also considered so worthless that it was thrown away like trash. Worse, the remains left inside the torn black garbage bag looked small and curled, almost childlike.

Dread flooded to her fingertips. Violent death was bad enough, but when children were involved, it became a special kind of hell for everyone involved.

Her gaze dropped to Matt, crouched at her feet and flanked by his students. He held the edges of the bag apart with gloved hands as they peered into the gloom.

"What can you tell me?" she asked.

Matt's eyes raised to hers, anger banked in their depths. "We need to get the victim back to the lab for a full examination, but we have enough to get started." He eyed the three young people clustered around him. "You've all had a look. What can you tell Leigh?"

"The victim is in the late bloat/early active decay stage," Paul said, his usual gregarious nature soberly curtailed. Leigh eyed him cautiously—in their previous case, he'd been the one with the weakest stomach. But, while pale, he looked steady as he met her eyes. "Normally, we'd want to calculate the accumulated degree days to figure out time since death, but everything is going to be thrown off by the ambient temperature at this site."

"The heat coming off this trash heap is amazing." Leigh eyed the pile. "Are they always like this?"

Matt nodded. "A lot of the heat produced is due to biological breakdown of organic matter from discarded food and chemical oxidation. It's not unusual for landfills to spontaneously combust from the heat produced. Since the surface heat dissipates into the surrounding air, you're only getting a small indication of what the middle of this pile must be like. But you can see how even surface heat will affect the victim's decay rate." He squinted up into the late afternoon sun blazing overhead with nothing to shelter them. "I warned you in the lab how conditions would combine, easily tripling or quadrupling normal decomp rates."

"So how will you determine time since death?"

"It's going to be a challenge. For a fresh victim, we'd use the more exact measurements of rigor mortis, livor mortis and liver temp. Considering these conditions, we'll have to make our estimates based on more theoretical science. But let's start at the beginning. Clearly the victim was stuffed in a garbage bag for both transport and concealment, and then dumped here. Fairly recently too, from the location. Another day or two, and I bet the bag would have been buried in more trash. Is there any way to find out when this load we're standing on was dumped?"

"I'll ask as soon as the victim is secured. The site manager is waiting for me. Maybe he can even identify which truck unloaded at this location, so we'll have an idea where it came from."

Matt shook his head. "I don't think that's how the bag got here."

"Oh." Leigh couldn't keep the disappointment out of her tone as she stared down at the remains. "I thought that would give us a solid starting point."

"I think it's unlikely. Look at this bag compared to the others around it."

Leigh instantly understood his point. The garbage around them spilled from torn bags. But the one containing their victim was virtually intact, pristine except for a few small tears and the long slash made by police after it was discovered. "You don't think this was ever transported in a trash compacting truck."

"No."

"If it was," Kiko interjected, "we'll see it in the bone structure. That kind of compaction pressure would easily break bones. If the skeleton is lacking postmortem fractures, then that's not how the bag got here."

Matt pushed to his feet, shading his eyes with a latex gloved hand as he scanned the perimeter. "Chain link fence, but it's got to be over six feet high. It would be tricky to climb that with a hundred plus pounds of dead weight on your back, but not impossible. Getting caught on the fence during the trip over would explain some of the small tears in the bag."

"If the body was carried into the site, then that tells us something about the murderer. It's doubtful the killer is a woman simply from a strength aspect," Leigh stated.

"I can't see this place being guarded at night," Paul said. "It's a trash heap. Who needs to protect garbage? Anyone could slip in after dark."

"More than that, it's a great way to get rid of a body," Leigh said. "This is just a small municipal landfill, essentially a trash transfer station. This garbage gets transferred to the bigger regional center in Haverhill where it's burned. Then the ash is permanently buried."

"Efficient. No body to identify and no way to trace any evidence back to you. If we hadn't been tipped off, it might actually have gone off without a hitch." Matt motioned her closer. "Come take a better look while the body is still *in situ*." He glanced down the mound of trash to where several Crime Scene Services techs stood waiting. "Then we'll get the techs up here for photos before we contain and move the remains."

The students stepped back to give them room. Matt crouched down, balancing on the balls of his feet while Leigh sank down beside him. For a moment her head swam as the pungent fumes, heavy with hydrogen sulfide and ammonia, simultaneously went to her head and her gut. The trash heap itself smelled horrible, but at this distance, the stench of putrefaction overwhelmed even it. Her stomach rolled in response and she looked up through watering eyes to find Matt's sympathetic gaze locked on her face. She turned away, willing her stomach to settle. When she turned back a moment later, her face was set and she gave Matt a brief nod before turning to her victim. He waved a hand at the mouth of the bag, scattering a cloud of flies into the air around them.

As the insects finally cleared, she scanned the contents of the torn black garbage bag. Strands of long, dark, tangled hair slithered from the tear in the bag. What remained of the body lay curled in the thick, frothy ooze puddled within the confines of the plastic. Leigh's lips tightened as she took in the bloated face, the skin sickly shades of green, orange and black. One eye was open, a thick white haze nearly obscuring the brown iris. The skin sagged from the naked torso, sloughing off in some sections to reveal liquefying tissue and pale bone beneath.

"We'll take samples from the collected fluids before we risk shifting the remains. We can analyze the breakdown products as one way of confirming postmortem interval." Matt indicated the large greasy stain soaked into the trash around the bag. "There's also been a lot of leakage so I'd like the techs to collect the trash under this area to a minimum depth of one foot. I doubt there will be any evidence there we don't already have, but once we release the site, we lose everything, so better safe than sorry."

"You can determine a timeline from the breakdown products?"

"Yes. When muscle and fat break down, volatile fatty acids are produced. The ratio of those compounds can indicate the decay stage. We'll need to keep the remains in Rowe's morgue until we're ready to macerate, so we'll also ask him about sampling vitreous fluids from the eye. Normally in an outdoor case like this, we'd also use insects to set time since death. Unfortunately, considering the closed bag, that likely won't be a possibility. But we'll watch closely for larvae when we examine the remains. There are a few small tears in the bag, likely from transport, so we may get lucky yet. Considering how the ambient temperature will have artificially accelerated decomp, they'd actually be our most accurate way to determine time since death, as long as the body was dumped shortly after death."

"So you can do a biochemical analysis and you might have bugs to work with. But that's all going to take time. Is there any way you can estimate time since death from just looking at the remains?" When Matt gave her a flat stare, she threw up both hands defensively. During their first case together, his reluctance to guess at postmortem interval had been only one in a string of disagreements between them. "I know—you need to be sure. Can you give me anything now, or is it simply too soon?"

Matt took a long moment to consider. "This is a rough estimate only, so when you're looking at missing person reports, be generous with the time period. Let's assume the body was dumped within twenty-four hours after the murder. So . . . given the conditions of the past week or so—the fact it's been Indian-summer warm and sunny, the heat from the landfill, and the fact it's still at the top of the heap—I'm going to estimate the body's been here for three to four days. A week max. But I think the manager of this facility will be able to narrow that range simply based on when trash was last dumped here." When Leigh started to speak, he held up an index finger to stop her. "I repeat, that's a rough estimate, so look for missing persons for up to three weeks. I can't see it being more than that simply because of where the remains were found, but what if they were stored for a while before being dumped? We can't discount that as a possibility."

"Works for me. Cause of death?"

Matt crouched down closer, squinting into the gloom. "I need a much better look than I'm getting while leaving the remains *in situ*, but I've been watching the flies around the body. They're concentrating heavily on the skull. They're going to be attracted to traumatic wounds, so I read that as an indication of local trauma. A head injury could be cause of death." He froze for a moment, and then leaned in further. "Someone hand me a flashlight."

Leigh leaned in closer, but couldn't see anything distinctive in the mass of putrefied flesh. "What do you see?"

"I'm not sure yet." Not taking his eyes off the remains, he held out his gloved left hand. Kiko pulled a flashlight from her pocket and flipped it on. She pressed it into Matt's open palm. Holding it in an overhand grip, he shone the light directly at the skull. Reaching in with his free hand, he gently pressed down on the lower jaw, his fingers sinking into the spongy tissue as the mouth opened fractionally. Pulling back his hand, he glanced up at Leigh. "Call up the tech with the camera. There's something in the mouth but we need photos before I go any further."

He stood and carefully climbed over to Paul, motioning him to turn around and then rooting around in the pack on Paul's back with his clean hand. He pulled out a set of slender forceps just as Leigh returned with the tech. "I need *in situ* photos of the mouth area," Matt instructed. "Then I'm going to see what's in there." He waited patiently while the tech snapped a series of photos. Once the remains were clear, he crouched down again.

Leigh stepped up behind him. "Hand me the flashlight. That way you'll have both hands free." She moved in close behind him, being careful to stay far enough back that she didn't hamper his movements in the close space. Sliding one hand under his arm, she directed the beam of light into the bag as she peered over his shoulder. Repeating his earlier movements, Matt gently opened the mouth and she leaned in, her chin slipping over his shoulder.

"Angle the light up a bit . . . perfect." Slipping the forceps in between the teeth, he fished for a moment and then started to draw out a narrow ribbon.

"What on earth—?"

"Keep that light up. I'm trying to keep it away from the tissue." Matt slid his free hand under the jaw to catch the ribbon as it finally came free, glistening in the light, shiny with dark fluids. "Kiko, grab a sample jar." He drew the ribbon into the light, where it hung from the forceps, the end coiled in his palm.

Leigh snapped off the flashlight as they all grouped together, staring at their first piece of evidence.

Red, white and blue ran in a single stripe down the length of the ribbon. Block letters repeated the words 'Merrimac Arms—5th Annual Veterans Bike Run' every few inches.

"It's one of those ribbons you tie onto your car antenna," Leigh said. "Like from Mothers Against Drunk Driving."

"But this one's for a motorcycle antenna," Paul said.

"Why do you say that?"

Paul pointed to the type on the ribbon. "It's a bike run. Get it? Not bicycle, but motorcycle. It's a charity event to raise money for military vets. I've never been to that one, but I did a few of them back home in New York City."

"You ride?"

"Sure. A guy's got to get around, and girls love a guy in leathers." He grinned when Kiko gave an unlady-like snort. "Well, some girls do."

"Not to mention it's more reasonable on a student salary," Matt said. "That's why I had a bike back in San Marcos."

Leigh gaze slid down Paul's body, from his slightly spikey hair, down over the Tyvek coveralls smeared with stains from the pile, to his heavy work boots. "You just don't look like the biker type to me."

"Like a Hell's Angel? Nah . . . there's a difference between a biker and someone who rides. It's transportation for me, but I know some guys who consider it a way of life."

"There's a reason that was planted on the body," Matt said.

"Whoever did it knew it would be found if the remains were ever discovered."

"Which makes you wonder if it was someone other than the murderer," Kiko said. "Surely he was banking on the remains never being found."

"All things to consider," Leigh agreed.

"Whoever made the ribbon can't spell," Paul commented. " 'Merrimack' is spelled with a 'k'. Like the River."

Kiko rolled her eyes. "Your city boy roots are showing again. It's not misspelled. 'Merrimac' is the historic name for the city of Lawrence."

"Then whoever named the river goofed," Paul quipped.

Ignoring Paul, Kiko held out the open, wide-mouthed sample jar. Matt carefully lowered the ribbon into it, and then capped it and wrote the evidence details on the label.

"Female, do you think?" Leigh indicated the hair slipping from the garbage bag.

"Long hair might make you lean in that direction. I can't tell from the facial features at this point, and the bloating of the torso makes it impossible to distinguish breast tissue when the remains are curled up, but there should be enough flesh remaining to determine genitalia. But once we've gotten all we can out of the flesh, I'll macerate the remains over the week-end using warm water and detergent to strip away the putrefying tissue and confirm biological sex from the bones. We'll also be able to study the bones for signs of injury. They'll tell an accurate tale of what happened."

"You don't . . . ." Leigh paused and then forced herself to spit out her greatest fear. "You don't think it's a child, do you?"

Matt looked up at her sharply and shook his head. "Not a small child, no. At worst, it might be a teenager."

Leigh's shoulders sagged as she blew out the breath she hadn't realized she'd been holding. "We had our fill of teenagers in the last case."

"Yeah, we did." He stood, and Leigh followed suit. "So . . . bikers, huh? A big muscular biker is exactly the kind of person who could haul a body over a chain link fence."

"Exactly what I was thinking. It's definitely the first thing on my list to look at." She turned and started down the pile of trash. "Now let's get the techs up here. It's time to get started."

CHAPTER THREE: BRACKETING

Bracketing: the process of taking multiple photographs of the same scene using different exposure settings. Bracketing is used when small changes in exposure cause large changes to the latent image and make it difficult for the photographer to capture the best possible image.

Saturday, 7:55 p.m.
Lawrence, Massachusetts

Leigh clutched Matt's waist tighter as he accelerated onto the onramp to the I-495. He grinned, enjoying the breathlessness of the wind and the rumble of a bike under him for the first time in years, but relishing Leigh's body pressed against his back like a second skin even more.

They were en route to the Merrimac Arms to spend Saturday night mixing with the locals and quietly asking questions as they followed their first lead. In order to stay under the radar, Matt talked Paul into lending them his motorcycle and his leather jacket for Leigh. Luckily Matt had a leather jacket of his own since Paul's slender frame was no match for Matt's broader, more muscular physique.

It had been a close call, with Paul wanting to go so badly himself he almost didn't agree.

"He wanted to do what?*" Leigh didn't even try to contain her incredulity.*

Matt pulled a helmet off the back of the bike, watching as Leigh shrugged into the black leather jacket, and then nodding in approval as it fit smoothly over her athletic body. "Some solo investigating. Kiko was taking great pleasure in describing how you were going to tear him limb from limb when you found out after the fact."

"She's not far off the mark. Paul's a little too into crime fighting. He needs to leave that for the cops."

"That's exactly what I told him. Just before I talked him into lending us his bike."

Leigh rolled her eyes. "You're almost as bad as he is."

He grinned, handing her the helmet and then picking up his own. "Yeah, but I get to tag along with the cop on her official business. That's entirely different."

"You keep telling yourself that." She eyed the bike suspiciously. "You're sure you remember how to ride this? I have no interest in ending up a bloody smudge on the interstate."

Matt secured his helmet and then swung one leg over the bike. "I haven't ridden in a while, but you don't forget how. Besides, I took it for a spin around the block to get a feel for it." He shifted the bike off the kickstand and patted the seat behind him. "Hop on."

"You say you have a license for this thing?"

"You and your licenses. Yes, I always renewed it, even after I sold my bike, just in case. Now quit stalling."

Bracing her hands on Matt's shoulders, she climbed on behind him, scooting forward so her thighs bracketed his. "Ah, now I get it. This is your version of a cheap date."

He turned and winked at her from behind his visor, the slightly raised backseat putting them eye-to-eye. "And now you've figured out my ulterior motive. Hold on tight." He waited while she slid her arms around him, getting a good grip on his leather jacket, and then they were roaring down the road.

They pulled into the parking lot of the Merrimac Arms fifteen minutes later, smoothly gliding to a stop at the end of a row of motorcycles. They got off and stowed their helmets.

Matt scanned the parking lot—the majority of the vehicles were bikes, but there were a healthy number of pickups too. Clearly, this wasn't the Mercedes crowd. He glanced over at Leigh, who was pulling out her low ponytail and shaking her blonde hair out over her shoulders. "Ready?"

"Yeah. Keep it casual in there. I don't want to let on that I'm a cop unless I have to." She adjusted her leather jacket, tugging it down over her hips. Matt had a brief flash of the Sig Sauer he'd seen in a shoulder holster before she'd covered it with the leather jacket back in Boston. *Just in case.*

Leigh started toward the door, but Matt caught her arm. "It's just . . ." He struggled to put what he'd been dwelling on during the ride into coherent words. "We have the ribbon and it points toward this place. But it also points straight toward veterans because of that charity bike race."

"It bothers you that a vet could be involved?"

"A bit. I know the majority of the people involved in that race are probably vets and their friends and families. Let's just not jump the gun. Remember these guys went through hell and back. Even if they're tattooed, biker tough guys, what they went through over there made them what they are today."

"And if it makes one of them guilty of murder?"

"Then we'll take him down because that's what he deserves. Just try to keep an open mind."

"Deal. Do you think the fact that you're a veteran will open some doors for us in there?"

"Maybe. We'll use it if we need to."

"I know you're not comfortable with it, but since nothing came up in my missing person searches for disappearances in this area over the past three weeks, that kind of leverage might come in handy. We need something to move in this case."

"By Monday I'll be looking at the bones themselves, and I'm sure we'll have something to work with there. But, in the meantime, here we are. Come on."

They crossed the parking lot. Matt held open the heavy wooden door, letting Leigh precede him. The pub was dim and music pumped with a ferocity that had the bass notes vibrating his sternum. A long, dark wood bar ran the length of the back wall, nested bottles sitting in neat rows in front of a mirror. A row of chrome and black leather stools hugged the bar, mostly occupied by a mixture of men and women in varying degrees of denim and leather. The *crack* of ricocheting billiard balls split the squeal of guitars as a pool game started over to their left. Wide screen TVs hung high on the walls, showing the Bruins' game.

Leigh nodded over at the bar. "Let's start over there."

Matt followed her to two empty stools next to a heavily bearded man wearing a black T-shirt with a stylized eagle, wings curved in an upward arc and razor sharp talons extended.

As the bartender slid their order of two draft beers across the bar, Leigh opened the conversation. "Is this the Merrimac Arms that hosts the bike race? The one for vets?"

The big man puffed out his chest and grinned. "It is. Been sponsoring it for years."

"We heard good things about it from a friend." Matt did his best to ignore the grime on the lip of his glass and took a swallow of beer, reminding himself that alcohol was sterilizing. "He rode in the last one. Said you had a good crowd."

The bartender picked up a damp rag—once probably white, but now a shabby gray—and started to wipe down the bar. Each swipe left a damp streak, but the surface didn't look any cleaner. "We did, didn't we, Colt?"

The man next to them raised his head, his empty shot glass wrapped in a meaty fist. "Last August? Sure did." He pushed the empty glass toward the bartender with an index finger. Without being asked, the bartender filled it with dark amber liquid from a bottle in the well, and the man downed it in one gulp. "Again."

Matt drained a quarter of his glass in a show of camaraderie. "Is it only vets that come out for it?"

"Mostly."

"Not so many women then?" Leigh asked, reaching past Matt to snag a handful of peanuts from the bowl on the counter.

"Wouldn't say that. Some partners and friends ride with us."

"So it's not just locals then." She popped several peanuts into her mouth.

"Nah. People come from all over. Even from out of state."

Matt's heart sank. If their victim had anything to do with out of town participants, tracking them down was going to be a real challenge. "How did you do last year?"

"Raised almost six thousand."

Matt raised his glass in a toast to their success. "Where does the money go?"

"Local veterans' association." Colt eyed Matt from under bushy eyebrows. "You're asking a lot of questions. Why the interest?"

"I like to see our boys get taken care of." He held out a hand. "Fifteenth Marine Expeditionary Unit. You?"

The big man shook hands. Matt clenched his jaw and forced his face to remain blank as the grip painfully ground the distal ends of his metacarpals together. "Army. Fourth Infantry Division."

"Iraq. Hell of a posting, man."

"No shit. Afghanistan?"

"Yeah. Here's to our boys." He tapped his glass against Colt's raised and magically refilled shot glass before draining it. "We're relatively new to the area and we heard good things about this place and the people here. Thought it might be good to check out."

"You heard right. You'll find good old American food and company here."

Leigh was sitting close enough that Matt felt her body go suddenly still. But when she spoke, her question was so casual that if he hadn't been touching her, he wouldn't have suspected she'd caught at a thread. "Is that hard to find around here?"

Colt leaned in conspiratorially and Matt's eyes watered at the blast of rot gut whiskey on his breath. "Let's just say that Lawrence has a little immigration problem."

Leigh braced her forearm on the railing, tipping her head intimately toward Colt. "Too many . . . foreigners?"

Matt could hear an edge of revulsion in Leigh's tone, but he doubted the biker caught the subtlety.

"*Way* too many." Colt's face darkened, his fist clenching on the surface of the bar. "We go over there and fight so they have a place to live. And what do they do? They come here and live in our towns and steal American jobs. We don't like it."

"We?"

"None of us." He turned to the group at the pool table. "Do we boys? We don't like spics and all those 'legal immigrants' taking our jobs."

A chorus of 'no's and colorful curses rumbled from the group.

Colt turned back to the bartender who was watching the group get rowdier with a nervous expression. "And we don't welcome them in this establishment, do we, Pete?"

"No, no we don't." Pete looked relieved when someone from the far end of the bar signaled for a drink. He scuttled away without another word, nervously glancing backwards only after he reached his next customer.

Matt swallowed the biting comment that rose to his lips and reached for the peanuts. He jammed a handful in his mouth, chewing viciously, but it still didn't overwhelm of the bitter taste of disgust on his tongue.

———

The door closed behind them with a thud, muffling the pounding music and leaving them in the sudden quiet of a cool, breezy fall night.

"Well . . . that kind of puts a new spin on things, doesn't it?" Matt said, taking his first easy breath in over an hour. He'd declined another beer, citing having to drive, but Colt had pulled him into a game of pool with his cronies. Leigh looked on, holding her own from the advances of the men around her, while he'd been soundly thumped. He hadn't put much effort into the attempt— better safe than sorry, and this group looked like it was walking a dangerous edge.

"I knew that Lawrence had a large immigrant population, but I didn't anticipate the locals having such an issue with it."

" 'Issue' makes it sound so minor. The more they talked, the more I realized their hatred goes bone deep. They honestly see the negative aspects of their world being the fault of people looking for a better way of life for themselves and their families."

"It wasn't all of them, though. A few of the guys either gave half-hearted responses or none at all. I get the feeling that there's real pressure to conform to the group leaders' views, and ethnicity definitely seems to be a hot button issue for some of them. Are you going to be able to give me an estimate of race when you look at the bones on Monday?"

"That little detail has been at the top of my 'to do' list for over an hour. We may have just found the motive for the murder. Not who, specifically, but possibly why. We need to identify the remains first, but if he or she wasn't a white American, then we need to see if we can connect the vic to someone here in Lawrence."

"More specifically, if we can connect the victim to someone who took part in the race. It's a charity event to raise money. That means someone has a list of all the participants. I need to get that list and then cross reference it against police records. Let's start with seeing who already has a record. If someone resorted to murder because of their hatred of immigrants, it's likely they've got something else on their sheet already." Leigh's gaze trailed back to the door of the pub. "One of those men could be the murderer. The only question is—which one?"

CHAPTER FOUR: COLLIMATION

Collimation: the process of correctly aligning all of the elements of a lens assembly to produce well-focused images. Collimation is often required after an assembly suffers severe thermal or mechanical shock.

Monday, 7:32 p.m.
Boston University, School of Medicine
Boston, Massachusetts

Matt sat at his desk with only the green-shaded banker's lamp on the corner throwing a soft glow over a flurry of papers and his open laptop. The rest of the room was draped in gloom.

Normally, the lab was a bustling hive of activity—grad students coming and going, undergraduate office hours, colleagues seeking advice, his own research. But now the lab was shadowed and silent.

He preferred it that way tonight. It suited his mood.

Chin propped on one fist, his eyes were fixed on his monitor as he flipped through photos. Some he glanced at briefly, others—often photos of the lost—held his attention for an extended moment before he moved on. He automatically picked up his coffee mug and raised it to his mouth, wincing as the ice-cold brew touched his lips. He set the mug down on the desk and pushed it away in disgust.

He turned at the sound of footsteps in the corridor, watching the door until it finally opened.

Leigh stepped through, her key card still in her hand. She froze, momentarily silhouetted by the light streaming in from the corridor, falling in an elongated rectangle over the floor. "Matt?"

Matt pushed back from the desk and stood. "Here."

Leigh closed the door behind her, throwing the lab back into darkness. Her eyes skimmed over what she could see of him, clearly confused. "I thought you wanted to show me the remains now you've defleshed the skeleton?"

"I do." He circled his desk to stand near the window, crossing his arms over his chest. His gaze flicked to the remains in the corner and then back to Leigh.

Her eyes scanned the darkened lab. "Where is everyone?"

"I sent them home."

"We've always done this as a group before."

How far they'd come that instead of questioning his students' presence, she now questioned their absence. "Not tonight. I didn't want them here for this." His tone was clipped and he cursed himself for not keeping a tighter hold on his emotions.

Uneasiness flashed across Leigh's face as wariness tightened her stance. "What's wrong?" She took two strides toward him, one hand extended, but then stopped as he involuntarily stepped back. "What's going on?"

"The case has taken a turn and I need to explain some things about our victim. But I need it to be only you. You need to know this information because it's crucial to the case, but I'm not ready to share this with everyone just yet. They'll need to know eventually . . . but not tonight."

Her head cocked in question, but she waited silently.

Matt blew out a breath, trying to shake off some of his tension, but it stubbornly clung to him, locked in his shoulders and in the greasy mass curdling in his stomach. "Okay, let's do this." He forced himself to cross the floor to the light switch beside the door.

Light flooded the lab and he turned around, blinking in the sudden glare to find her staring at him warily. "Look, I'm sorry about all the cloak and dagger stuff," he said.

"Are you in trouble?" Leigh's voice was flat, but her eyes were sharply assessing him for anything amiss. Cop's eyes.

The question brought him up short. "Why would I be in trouble?"

"Because of the cloak and dagger stuff. Do you need help?"

Matt let out a rough laugh. "No, nothing like that. It's just that . . . well . . . maybe it's best I just show you." He led her over to a gurney, the one he'd pushed into the corner. *So much for out of sight, out of mind.* "Here she is."

Leigh came to stand beside him at the side of table where they could look at the pale bones together. Laid out in anatomical order, the bones told a startling story of sudden, violent death.

"Confirming what we theorized from the fleshed remains days ago, it's a woman. A young woman. I'd place her in her late teens to early twenties, maybe twenty-two or -three at most, but more in the range of eighteen to twenty."

Leigh circled the table to stand at the head, looking down at the shattered skull. Six sharp-edge pieces lay in a halo around the jagged-topped cranium. "So you were right at the scene—cause of death was a blow to the head. A single blow?"

"Yes. There's more damage than just that, but a single blow was what killed her."

"Can you identify the weapon?"

"Yes, but before we get into that, I want to show you something else. Something so subtle I almost missed it."

"Okay . . ." She drew the word out slowly, and even though he wasn't looking at her, he could feel her gaze on him, curiosity and concern intermingled.

He carried the skull in his gloved hands to the nearby bench. He flipped on the brilliant ring-light encircling a large magnifying lens on a telescoping arm. "Come look at this." He held the skull under the lens, tipping it so she could see the delicate nasal bones. He pointed to the small, uneven bony growth that rimmed the edge of the bones. "You see this small growth of lamellar bone along the rim of the nasal aperture, going down on both sides over the frontal process of the maxilla?" He ran an index finger from the top of the nasal opening down toward the bottom.

Leigh leaned in, going up on tip-toe for a better view. "Yes."

"That indicates healing after bone damage."

"Her nose was broken?"

"Not exactly. A nasal fracture would have traveled deeper into the nasal bones and the maxilla." He turned the skull in his hands, this time holding the side of the skull up to the lens. "See here, over the supramastoid crest, the mastoid portion and the typanic part surrounding the external acoustic meatus?"

"English, Matt. I'm not one of your students." She softened her words by laying her hand on his arm and giving it a gentle squeeze.

"Right, sorry. See the bony structures around the ear canal?"

"It's kind of hard to see, but am I looking at more extra bone?"

"Yes."

"What caused it?"

"Injury. This is the bone remodeling after healing. It's the remnants of the cartilage callus and later the lamellar bone that overlaid it. Given enough time it would have remodeled to be almost invisible."

"So this is an old injury then? Is it relevant?"

"Very much so, I'm afraid." He turned the skull over and silently held it up for her.

Leigh leaned in and then went very still. "This side of the skull has the same signs of injury and healing."

"Yes." He carefully set the skull back down on the gurney, the empty eye sockets staring sightlessly out from under the horrible gash in the top of the cranium. When he turned to Leigh, she was standing in the same place, hands on her hips, staring at the skull.

"These injuries mean something to you?" she asked.

"Yes."

"This is what you wanted me to see without the students."

He nodded.

"Why?"

"I've seen this injury before in Afghanistan, but when I saw it, it was fresh."

Understanding dawned in her eyes. She knew many of his memories of his time as a medic with the Marines in Afghanistan following 9/11 were still raw; he kept those memories private except to a very special few.

"Tell me," she said simply.

Sudden exhaustion washed through him and he dropped into the desk chair in front of Paul's cluttered workstation, under one of the dark windows. "It happened after we took Kandahar. We pulled back to Camp Rhino for a few days. I met Sayeda when she was brought into camp. She was badly injured and the man with her was afraid she'd bleed out if he took her all the way to Kandahar. When they arrived, Sayeda was wearing the traditional burqa and chadri head-covering the Taliban require of women. But her chadri was soaked in blood."

Leigh made a small sound, but he carried on as if he hadn't heard.

"We had one of the local women assisting as part of our nursing staff and she was able to translate so we could find out what happened to the girl, and then explain how we would treat her. It took ages to get Sayeda to lift the chadri to so we could evaluate the damage." He shifted restlessly in the chair and then looked up to meet Leigh's eyes. "She was nearly beaten to death, and her nose and her ears had been cut off. It's a favorite practice of the Taliban." Matt's gaze slid back to skull on the cold stainless steel. "And that's exactly what's happened here."

For a moment Leigh was so stunned she couldn't speak. "Why would they care about one woman? I thought they considered them to be second-class citizens."

"You're right. By and large, women are beneath their notice. It was Sayeda's husband who mutilated her."

"Why would he do such a thing?" Leigh's tone rose, edged with horror and disbelief.

"She was married to a much older man when she was just ten years old in a practice known as *baad*. She was payment for a debt between the families, and from that early age on she was essentially a slave to the man and his other wives. She was beaten regularly and forced into sexual relations with her husband when she was much too young." Fury rose at the memory and he forced himself to slowly pull in a deep breath. "She feared for her life, so she tried to run away. Unfortunately, one of the favored wives caught her and brought her back to their husband."

"And that was her punishment? The beating? And the mutilation?" Leigh started to pace the floor, outrage leaching out of her in nervous energy.

Matt nodded. "A wife who tries to leave her husband not only shames herself, but the whole family. After a lot of coaxing, she finally told us her husband cut off her nose and ears with a knife, and then beat her within an inch of her life. They drove her out into the desert and abandoned her with no food or water, hoping she'd quietly die alone out there."

"Barbaric," Leigh whispered.

"Sayeda was one of the lucky ones. She managed to find the strength to crawl to a nearby settlement, and one of the women there convinced her husband to bring Sayeda to us for treatment. Many other women are not so lucky; those are the ones who die alone in the shadows." His eyes went hard. "The Taliban also do this as punishment for men who help the U.S. military or interfere with the opium trade, and as a reminder to those who vote in elections. But it is also considered an acceptable practice in tribal society as punishment for a woman who is disobedient."

"The intention being that you will forever show the world the face of your shame? Or, in some ways, simply be considered faceless?"

"Yes."

"It's barbaric and it's cruel. That poor girl. And it must have been horrible to treat her."

"We did what we could, but we weren't plastic surgeons. And this wasn't a clean transection; she'd been hacked. We stabilized her and made her as comfortable as we could, then medivaced her to Kandahar for better treatment. She needed a hospital, not a newly established Marine camp. And it wasn't safe there. We could have been Taliban targets at any moment."

"Another great memory of the war for you."

He gave a rough laugh. "They're not all bad . . . just most of them."

She surprised him by stepping between his spread thighs and running one hand over his hair, her thumb briefly brushing the scar at his temple—a souvenir from later in that same campaign. He leaned his head against her abdomen and allowed himself a moment of comfort as her fingers threaded through his hair.

"Thank you for sharing this with me," she said quietly. "Now I understand why you wanted to keep this private."

He tipped his head back to meet her eyes. "I know this information will make a big difference in who you're looking for." Not wanting to dwell on the past and what it represented, he steered them back to the case. "But think hard about what you saw. Those wounds were healed. Likely for about six months from the progression of the remodeling."

The hand resting lightly on his shoulder suddenly gripped hard, her short nails biting into his flesh. When she finally spoke, her voice was low and tight with anger. "You're telling me that those injuries aren't associated with her death? That she lived at least half a year with that face?"

"Or lack of one, yes."

"But that means . . ." She strode away from him, back to the gurney. "If she'd gone out in public like that, missing her nose and her ears, someone would have noticed. Even if she wore a head scarf and something to cover her face, the lack of a nose would still be noticeable. If anyone questioned her or informed the authorities, her assault would have been investigated. Whoever did it couldn't possibly take that chance. She must have lived in terrible isolation after her injuries, possibly with no one but the person who did this. She'd have been a virtual prisoner."

"Exactly. Also, I suspect no one ever reported her missing, so you won't find her that way. I think what we're looking at here is someone who immigrated to America from Afghanistan, maybe with her family, maybe with a husband. I can test for this—I can look at strontium levels in various bones to determine where in the world she grew up and where she's been for the past six years. But there's no way she traveled here like that unnoticed, so my money is on it happening after she got here. It's possible she's from some other country in Central Asia or the surrounding area, but to my knowledge, this is a practice that's strictly Taliban-oriented. This is the group you need to look at. If a young woman suddenly disappeared six months or more ago, surely someone must have noticed."

"So I need to look for immigration records from Central Asia dating back further than six months."

"Yes. Also, Kiko has offered to do a 2D facial reconstruction of the victim. Having a face to work with might help, especially if it's someone who's been off the radar for a while. And there's something else that occurred to me. Remember how the body was found naked?"

"Yes."

"If we're talking about Afghan women, they're traditionally always covered up while out in public, especially their heads and faces. Which makes me think that it's significant that she was found that way."

"Could be indicative of the fact that they no longer considered her a part of their group. Maybe they were distancing themselves from her? Or it could be they simply didn't want any connection back to their community."

"Maybe. Now, back to the remains." He indicated two ribs on the right side with an index finger. "Ribs seven and ten are both fresh fractures. So is her left ulna." He pointed to a bone in the lower arm, snapped cleanly through.

"She was beaten before being killed?"

"Yes. Unfortunately, with the body in that condition, we lost most of the soft tissue injuries to decomposition, but I bet there were other contusions as well." He moved to the far side of the table and picked up a humerus. "I also see signs of long term abuse." He pointed to a healed break in the upper bone of the arm. "This fracture has healed and is well into the process of remodeling, but it wasn't set properly, so now the bone has a permanent bend in it. If she was an immigrant, it could have been set back in her home country."

"Or maybe it was set here, but not at a hospital? As poor immigrants with no health care maybe they couldn't afford treatment."

"Not buying it," Matt said. "There are still places they could have gone for such a severe injury—a county hospital for example. I think it was set at home so no outsider knew about it."

"You're suggesting domestic abuse," Leigh said flatly.

"Yes." Matt picked up the skull again, angling it toward her and pointing into the left eye socket. "There's a healed break here, in the orbital surface of the maxilla. It's commonly called an orbital floor fracture and it's one of the more common domestic abuse injuries." Setting down the skull, he balled one gloved fist and threw a slow punch at Leigh, stopping more than an inch from her left eye. "It's called 'retropulsion theory'. When something larger than the eye socket forcibly strikes it, the intraocular pressure builds up, fracturing the bony floor under the eyeball." He turned back to the victim on the table. "She was hit like that at least once, but it could have been multiple times if the other strikes didn't fracture bone. There are also signs of broken fingers in the past. And then there's the cause of death."

"Clearly, it was a blow to the head."

"It was. But it's also a little more than that once you reconstruct the details concerning the moment of death." He indicted the gaping wound on the top of the skull. "The skull is about 6mm thick at this point. The force required to not only fracture but totally displace this amount of bone is considerable. When the brain was intact, these fragments lay depressed below the plane of the adjacent bones. We're not talking about radiating fractures, this was pure force." He turned over several of the pieces; each of them was darkly stained. "As you can see from the underside staining, there was a considerable hematoma at the impact sight. She was hit *hard*."

"Have you got a feel for the weapon?"

"I'm leaning toward something circular and probably about one and a quarter inches in diameter. We swabbed the impact site for trace materials, so we're waiting for confirmation, but I think it was likely a metal pipe, probably a weapon of convenience."

"Nothing like a crowbar or tire iron?"

"Those would be too narrow. But the important thing here is the position of the blow." Raising a hand, he chopped a straight line down the center of his head. "Like this."

Leigh opened her mouth to speak, then snapped it closed again.

Head tilted, she stared at the spot he'd indicated before looking back at the bones. "How tall was she?"

She's got it. "About five-foot-five."

She reached out toward the skull, her ungloved fingers stopped just an inch short of contact. "And the blow is flat across the top of her skull, not on an angle. Even if the attacker was over six feet tall, the blow would still be at an angle."

"Right."

"And the blow was full force, like the kind you'd have if you had time and space for the momentum in a full arm swing." She pantomimed bringing a pipe down hard, the blow stopping at her hips.

He loved her quick mind and the way she could visualize the crime based on the raw data he gave her from the evidence spread before them. "Yes."

"God damn it, she was on her *knees*?" The hand holding the imaginary pipe clenched into a white-knuckled fist. "On her knees, begging for her life? Or mercy?"

"Or forgiveness," Matt added. "But yes, that's how I read the evidence. She'd been beaten and then she was killed by one hard blow to the skull, while she was on her knees in front of her attacker. Leigh, as bad as those bikers were on Saturday night, I don't think they're responsible for this. Yes, this could be considered a forced execution pose, but I don't think this was that cold or unemotional. I think this was done by someone much closer to the victim. Someone who'd been escalating her abuse for a prolonged period of time until he finally killed her."

Leigh turned away from her victim to pace the lab in agitation as she worked through the information in her head. Matt stripped off his gloves, leaving her to the privacy of her thoughts for a moment. This was the reason he'd been sitting in the dark, his mood spiraling into darkness—the combination of painful memories of the past and the horror of what this young woman must have suffered for at least the last six months of her life before being released by violent death. Beaten, bloody, alone. Seeing Leigh's fury lightened his heart just a little.

Whoever had done this was going to pay. They'd make sure of it.

CHAPTER FIVE: CHIAROSCURO

Chiaroscuro: an Italian word meaning "light-dark", it is the technique of using bold contrast in light and shadow to create the illusion of three dimensions in painting, photography, or cinematography. The chiaroscuro look is characterized by vaults of darkness containing subjects illuminated by soft pools of light.

Tuesday, 3:57 p.m.
Cambridge Kabobs Restaurant
Cambridge, Massachusetts

Leigh pushed through the door of the restaurant and was met by a wave of fragrant scents: baking bread, grilled meat, and a complex mixture of spices, including garlic, cardamom, and red pepper. Her mouth watered and her stomach grumbled, as if remembering the small smoothie she'd inhaled on the run four hours earlier. Even though it was mid-afternoon on a work day, the restaurant was still half-full, and Leigh glanced longingly at a table of diners, their platters loaded with thick kabobs and steaming rice.

Leigh had started her morning at a local resource center for Afghan women. It was an unexpectedly rude awakening—her heart bled to hear the stories of women and children who'd escaped Afghanistan full of hope for a better life in America, only to find the domestic abuse and harsh attitudes they'd fled followed them to their new home. The center provided a safe space to escape that abuse, as well as programs to educate women and their children, paving the way for a better life. When the workers at the resource center were not able to help with a potential victim ID—to the best of their knowledge, none of their clients were missing—they suggested a trip across the Charles to Cambridge. A significant Afghan population lived and thrived in that area, mainly within the restaurant business.

Leigh had spent the remainder of the morning and much of the afternoon visiting Afghani restaurants, but so far had come up empty. No one knew of any missing young women, especially one that mysteriously disappeared about six months before. And now, here she was starting again.

Maybe the fifth time's the charm?

Unlike some of the other establishments that emphasized multi-course meals served in a heavily ethnic setting, this restaurant was clearly the Afghani fast food equivalent with a 1950s diner feel—lots of light and chrome, with cheerful American music blasting through the speakers and the all-female staff behind the counter dressed down in jeans.

Leigh approached the counter. The dark-eyed woman behind the cash register greeted her with a hundred-watt smile. "What can I get you?" Her words were heavily accented, but her English was clear and well-enunciated.

Leigh cast a wistful glance at the heaps of steaming food behind the main counter before palming her badge and holding out the gold shield. "I'm Trooper Abbott from the Massachusetts State Police. I'd like to ask the owner some questions."

"I'm the owner." She turned to the brightly lit kitchen. "Najia, please take the register." She indicated a table near the wall. "Come, sit."

Leigh waited until they were both seated. "I'm looking for some information for my current investigation."

The woman narrowed her dark eyes. "Has one of my girls gotten into trouble? They know how we work—I offer employment, but they have to go to school and learn English. If one of them—"

"It's not one of your girls," Leigh cut her off. "At least as long as they're all accounted for, Ms . . ."

"Nazar. Farah Nazar."

"And you own *Cambridge Kabobs*?"

"Yes."

"If you don't mind me saying, that seems unusual within the Afghan community. I've been to several Afghani restaurants this morning and every one of them was run by a man with a mostly male staff."

Farah drew herself up, her eyes shining with pride. "The men say we women are not capable of independence, of running our own businesses. I prove them wrong. No man works under this roof. My girls and I, we run a good restaurant and make good food. And we have a loyal clientele to show for it." Her gaze drifted around her restaurant, her lips curved in a smile, raising her hand in a wave as she recognized a familiar face.

"I notice you wear American clothes and don't cover your hair."

Farah ran a hand over the flirty ends of her dark bob. "When in America, live like an American. I will not hide behind the hijab because some man tells me I must."

Leigh warmed to this brash, independent woman. Many of the women she met throughout the morning had been timid, and reluctant to talk unless granted permission by their husbands. Farah Nazar could not have been more different. "Good for you. It sounds like you know this community well. I'm working a murder case—the body of a young woman was found a few days ago, but we think she was killed within the last few weeks."

Farah sat back in her chair, her eyes serious. "You believe she was Afghani?"

"Yes."

The woman was quiet for a moment, save for the steady drum on her fingers on the tabletop. "I cannot think of anyone who is missing."

"It's actually a little more complicated than that. We think she actually disappeared from public view about six months ago, but wasn't killed until recently. Do you know of anyone who disappeared that long ago? She was probably in her late teens, but might have been as old as twenty-two or twenty-three."

Farah opened her lips to speak, but then suddenly froze, a look of stunned horror on her face.

Leigh leaned forward, her heart rate kicking up a notch in anticipation. "You know someone who fits that description?"

Ignoring the question, the other woman swiveled in her seat, her laser sharp gaze zeroing in on someone in the kitchen. "Aliah, come here, please." When a young woman looked up from mixing dough, Farah repeated her name, gestured, and then said something in what Leigh assumed was her native tongue. Farah turned back to face Leigh. "Aliah has only been in America for less than a year and her English is still not good. May I speak to her in Pashto?"

"Yes, but please translate both the question and the answer for me."

"Of course."

The young woman approached the table, giving Leigh a shy smile and Farah a small head bob. Farah launched into several rapid fire questions. Aliah looked frightened, until it became clear that Farah was trying to set her at ease as her words slowed and her tone gentled. Then the girl finally answered in the same language.

"I asked if she remembered anyone who disappeared from the community approximately six months ago," Farah said. "She confirmed my thoughts. A girl named Hoor Ahmadi used to be a regular in the neighborhood. Her family moved here . . . maybe as much as five or six years ago. She graduated from the local high school more than a year ago and has been working in her family's restaurant since then. But it's been a long time since we've seen her. Aliah says she's gone overseas. That is all she knows." Farah dismissed the girl to return to the kitchen with a few words and a wave of her hand.

Leigh had her notebook out and was scribbling fast. "What's the name of the restaurant?"

"*Ghazna.*" Disgust dripped from her tone.

Leigh slowly raised her head, taking in the curl of Farah's lip and the angry glint in her eye. "You have a problem with the restaurant?"

"Not the restaurant, although I think they could prepare more flavorful food. The owner. Tariq Ahmadi." She spat out a word in Pashto so strong Leigh didn't need a translator to discern her meaning.

"Ahmadi. That's the same last name as the girl. This is her father?"

"Yes."

"You've had problems with him?"

"Not at first. His brother came to America about ten years ago and settled in New York City. Opened a popular restaurant. Seeing the possibility of a better life for his family, Tariq followed him a few years later, settling here in Cambridge due to the larger Afghan population. I think he wanted the culture of home, but the opportunity of America. However, I suspect things spun out of his control."

"Like what?"

"His business—it started out well, but as more restaurants opened, his fell out of favor. His family—he desperately wants his children to learn their own culture, to hold onto it and value it as he does, but they just want to fit in with their friends. And that means leaving the old ways behind. A man like Tariq would see that as a betrayal."

"So it has caused problems between Mr. Ahmadi and his children?"

"I would imagine so, but he doesn't share his feelings with me. We used to be somewhat friendly, although he never approved of my running my restaurant because he believes every woman should answer to a man and I answer to no one. But over the years he has become more disagreeable, more angry, as the way of life he envisioned slipped through his fingers." She scowled, a quick flash of narrowed eyes and tight lips. "I've heard he talks badly about my restaurant, likely in hopes I will close down and go home to become some man's servant. Luckily enough, my food speaks for itself. He cannot hurt me."

Leigh set down her notebook, studying Farah thoughtfully. "He had a teenage daughter who went to the local high school and probably wanted to fit in with any friends she made there. How she acted, how she dressed would change accordingly."

"And would not be well received at home. Like most Afghan men, Tariq considers himself the undisputed head of the family.

He dictates how his women behave and demands they wear the chadri in public at all times. His wife is allowed to simply cover her head in the restaurant, but if she ventures outside, she must be hidden from view. His daughter as well."

"I can't see that sitting well with a girl adapting to life as an American. You mentioned his 'children'. He has a son or another daughter?"

"A son. Much younger than the sister. I see him occasionally. *He* is allowed to dress however he pleases."

"Charming double standard." Leigh held out her hand. "Thank you; you've been very helpful. If I have any other questions, I'll be in touch." She put one of her business cards down on the table. "Please feel free to call me if you hear or remember anything else you think might be useful."

The women stood.

"Will you go to *Ghazna* now?" At Leigh's nod, Farah smiled, but there was no joy in it, only vengeance. "Good luck to you then. If he did anything to his daughter, I hope he is punished. He is in America now. He would get away with that at home, but not here."

"No," Leigh agreed. "Not here, because now he has to deal with me."

―――――

Tuesday, 4:48 p.m.
Ghazna Restaurant
Cambridge, Massachusetts

Ghazna was nearly empty this late in the afternoon; only an older couple in Western clothes sat at a small table near the window.

A dark-skinned young man dressed in a long, embroidered tunic approached Leigh with a welcoming smile as she stood just inside the door. "Table for one?"

"Massachusetts State Police. I'd like to speak to Tariq Ahmadi."

Forehead wrinkled in confusion, the young man stepped back a pace. "Tariq is in the back. I will get him for you." Turning, he strode down the long aisle into the kitchen at the back of the restaurant, the door lazily swinging shut behind him.

Leigh took a moment to absorb her surroundings. The room was flanked with booths, chocolate-brown leather benches on each side of dark wood tables. Freestanding leather dining chairs and tables filled the center of the room. At the far end, a bar of cultured ledgestone was topped with slick black granite. Framed pictures hung on the walls including the famous photograph by Steve McCurry of a young Afghani girl with a rust colored headscarf and hauntingly vibrant green eyes.

Suddenly the door to the right of the bar eased open and Leigh caught a glimpse of a brightly lit office as a small head peered through the gap. It was a young boy, maybe ten or eleven years of age, dressed in a T-shirt and jeans. He nervously scanned the restaurant, his gaze resting briefly on Leigh before moving on. Then he retreated into the office, silently closing the door behind him.

An older man appeared at the kitchen door. He wore a plain navy blue tunic over loose pants and a small knit skull cap. He was followed by a woman in long flowing robes, a matching headscarf pulled discreetly low on her forehead so not even the crown of her head showed. Her eyes stayed locked on the carpet at the man's heels.

"I am Tariq Ahmadi," he said. "May I help you?"

"Trooper Leigh Abbott from the Massachusetts State Police." Making a snap decision to test a theory, Leigh held out her hand. The man's gaze flicked down to her hand but instead of shaking, he calmly folded his hands together and stared at her. Point proven, Leigh let her hand fall. "I'm looking for some information concerning a missing person."

The man waited patiently, his face impassive.

"You've run this restaurant for a few years?" she asked.

"I have."

"I've heard excellent things about it. It must be a full-time job and then some to run a popular restaurant like this."

"It is."

"You must have help."

"I do."

Leigh smiled patiently, ignoring the man's taciturn answers. She could do this all day if he wanted to play it that way. "Maybe your wife helps you?" Over Tariq's shoulder, the woman's head came up an inch, her gaze rising to meet Leigh's through her eyelashes. "Ma'am, do you help run the restaurant?"

"She does," her husband interjected.

Leigh purposely stepped sideways so the woman came fully into view. "I'd like to hear it from you, please." She repeated her question.

"Yes." The woman's voice was quiet, her eyes downcast again.

"Do your children also help?" Leigh pressed.

"Our son helps in the kitchen sometimes, but he is only twelve and is still learning. We have a very competent staff."

"What about your daughter?"

The thread she needed to tug was there in the mother's wide eyes and blanched skin. But it was the father who spoke. "How do you know about our daughter?"

"We're investigating a murder, and there is the possibility the victim may have come from the Afghan community. I came to Cambridge since it's one of the largest Afghani communities in the state. Your daughter's name came up."

"When was this murder committed?"

"We think within the past week, but we're still confirming."

"Hoor is a good and faithful daughter. She helped when she was here, but she returned home to Kabul months ago. It is not possible that she is your murder victim."

Leigh pulled out her notebook and flipped it open. "How long ago?"

"I'm not certain, but it must have been—"

His wife's quiet voice cut him off. "The end of April."

"And she hasn't returned?" Leigh asked.

"She went home to help my mother," Tariq said. "She is elderly and requires assistance, but doesn't want to leave her home yet. She will join us within the year so I can take care of her properly as a son should."

"Hoor doesn't need to be here for school?"

"She completed high school. That is all the schooling she requires. She was working for us, supporting the family. Now she is supporting the family at home. When it is time, she will return to help the family here once again."

Leigh decided to press a little harder. "Are you training her to take over once you retire?"

Tariq's horror telegraphed through his slack jaw and disbelieving eyes. "A woman in business?" His expression twisted as if the thought left him with a bad taste in his mouth. "That is a man's responsibility. I have a son. He will take over when it is time."

She knew she was baiting him, but she couldn't resist a parting jab. "Ms. Nazar at *Cambridge Kabobs* is a woman running her own business. It was very busy when I was there—" Leigh let her gaze roam over the nearly empty restaurant, her implication unspoken, but very much felt apparently, judging by the angry narrowing of Tariq's eyes. "—so she seems to be holding her own." She let her gaze settle back on his flushed face. "Thank you for your time, Mr. and Mrs. Ahmadi. I'll let you know if I have any other questions."

As she strode down the sidewalk, Leigh pulled her cell phone from her pocket and entered a now familiar speed dial number. "Hey, it's me. Are you at the lab still or are you heading home? Can I meet you there? I want to give you an update. I think we just hit pay dirt."

CHAPTER SIX: ZOETROPE

Zoetrope: an early attempt to create moving pictures by mounting a sequence of still images on the inside of a rotating, cylindrical drum having vertical slits cut along the upper edge. An observer looked through the slits at the photographs on the opposite side of the cylinder while spinning the drum. The shutter-like effect of the moving slits prevented the images from blurring together, and the rapid succession of images exploited human visual persistence to produce the illusion of motion.

Tuesday, 5:20 p.m.
Lowell Residence
Brookline, Massachusetts

Leigh was just stepping onto Matt's porch when his SUV pulled into the driveway. She waited as he got out of the vehicle and took the stairs two at a time to join her.

"Sorry, I had to finish up a few things before I could leave." Matt unlocked the front door and then followed Leigh inside. He shut the door behind them and dropped his keys into the wooden bowl on the foyer table. "Can you stay for dinner?"

"I'd love to, but I have to get back up to the Unit. I just wanted to do a quick run through with you while I was in town."

"Have time for coffee then?"

"That I can do."

Leigh sat at the kitchen table and outlined her day to Matt as he made coffee and then leaned against the counter, listening as it brewed. He poured two mugs and carried them over to the table.

"So the first thing to check is whether the girl really left the country," Leigh continued.

"Can Immigration tell you that?" Matt asked.

"Yes. You can't cross the border these days without some kind of paperwork and that's all recorded. If there's no record of her leaving the country, then that's a point in our favor."

"You made some great headway today. It certainly—" Matt stopped at the sound of a quiet whine coming from the empty doorway. Eyes suddenly narrowed, he swiveled in his chair. "Dad?"

There was a moment of silence and then Matt's father rolled into view from the hallway, a sheepish look on his tanned face and a big, ruddy Belgian Malinois at his side. The dog took one look at Leigh and immediately trotted across the room to her.

Laughing, she stroked her hands through his thick fur as he practically danced with excitement under her touch. Once an Army K-9 in Iraq before being caught in an explosion, Teak was now the faithful companion of a man confined to a wheelchair after the car accident that took not only his mobility, but the life of his wife. Leigh looked over to see Matt's father watching them with amusement. "Nice to see you, Mike."

"Good to see you too." Mike looked over at his son, only to find Matt staring at him levelly. "Something wrong?"

"Outed by your own dog." Matt shook his head in mock disgust. "How long were you out there listening?"

"Not . . . too long." Mike glanced sideways at Leigh. "Okay, I heard the whole thing. Your cases fascinate me. I know I'm not on the team so I shouldn't be privy to that information, but Matt shared the details of the damage to the victim's skeleton and I admit that curiosity got the better of me. You know how boring life can be for an old man when you're stuck at home in a wheelchair . . ." He gazed at her with pleading eyes.

Leigh laughed and patted him on the arm. "Laying it on a little thick, aren't you? You had me until your 'boring life'. Wheelchair or not, you're one of the most active, social men I know. Hell, you're in better shape than *I* am."

Mike chuckled. "Didn't think I could fool you, but it was worth a shot. And it wasn't all an act. I do find your cases fascinating."

"No point in closing the barn door after the horse is out," Leigh muttered. She nailed Matt with a pointed glare. "Shared the details of the skeletal damage, did you?"

Matt had the good grace to blush. "Well . . . yeah. You didn't mind during our first case. And from the moment I walked in the house that night, he knew something was up. So we talked it out."

"Fair enough, I suppose, considering." Leigh turned back to Mike. "Come on in. You might be able to add some insight to the conversation. But no case details ever leave this house, or Kepler will have my head."

"Scout's honor." Mike wheeled up to the open side of the table and Teak settled happily on the floor between his owner and Leigh.

Matt got up and poured his father a cup of coffee before joining them at the table again. "Hoor Ahmadi is certainly the right age for our victim, but I'd like medical records to corroborate antemortem fractures." His gaze snapped to Leigh over the rim of his coffee cup. "Wait a minute. You said she recently graduated from a local high school?"

"Yes."

"Do you know which one?"

"I don't, but I know of several people who probably do."

"If she recently graduated, then she might have a graduation picture in the school yearbook. Could you get a copy of it?"

"The parents certainly aren't about to help me, but I'll bet the school—" Leigh cut herself off as comprehension dawned and set her mug down on the table with a sharp rap. "Kiko's reconstruction. You want to do a comparison."

"Yes. But I don't want Kiko to see it beforehand. I don't want anything influencing her. I've seen what she's done so far. It's very good, but it's not finished. I'll have her work solely on that and she'll finish it tomorrow. If her drawing matches the face in that yearbook . . ."

"Then we have ourselves a victim to work with and that will give us the leverage we need for a warrant for her medical records. Or for DNA testing. They say she's been gone for six months, but if she's really been dead only a week or two, then her DNA should be all over wherever they kept her and we can match it to the remains."

"Assuming what you're looking for is everyday DNA," Matt said. "Hair, skin cells etcetera. If you're looking for the kill site, they may have cleaned it by now and while we might find traces of blood, if they used bleach, we might not be able to isolate enough intact DNA for PCR identification."

"There's no way she was kept at the restaurant," Mike said. "That's too public if Matt's theory about what they did to her is correct. They must have kept her at home."

"That would be my guess," Leigh agreed.

"If we don't find her DNA there," Matt said, "can you get a warrant for DNA samples from the father, mother and brother? Immediate family like that is almost always a good match."

"Definitely. I'll get that at the same time I get a warrant to search their home. I'll get a warrant for the restaurant as well, but I can't imagine finding anything of use there. Too public as Mike said."

Mike's expression darkened, and Leigh realized how similar father and son were in that moment; she'd seen that exact look on Matt's face on more than one occasion. "It's unbelievable what they did to her," the older man said. "You think it was the father?"

"I think there's a very good chance, especially after meeting him. He's not exactly waving the flag for women's lib. Also, if anyone outside of the family did that to her, they'd have reported the attack. But they covered it up, covered *her* up for months. And the mother's reaction was telling. She didn't react like her daughter was safely overseas. When I asked about Hoor, she was startled. In fact, I think I saw fear."

"Fear of being caught?"

"By us or by her husband. Remember our victim showed signs of domestic abuse. The wife could also be an abuse victim. And she might fear losing her way of life if her husband is arrested. Afghan woman are often treated as second-class citizens, so she might not realize her own strength and independence until it's tested." Leigh took another sip of coffee. "One thing is for sure, when I asked when Hoor had gone back to Afghanistan, the father hesitated and the mother knew the answer like—" Leigh snapped her fingers.

"I bet that's when the daughter was mutilated," Mike said. "Of course she'd remember it. The father's hesitation is telling though. Clearly that moment didn't mean anything to him."

"There's that second-class citizen thing again," Matt said, disgust in his voice.

"There's another possibility," Leigh said. "What if her disfigurement wasn't done by someone inside the family, but by someone outside the family who intended to put pressure on them in a way they can't admit to?"

Matt sat forward in his chair, staring at Leigh with narrowed eyes. "What do you mean?"

"What if it's the Afghan equivalent of a loan shark breaking your fingers when you're behind in your payments? What if money or some kind of debt is owed and they aren't paying it back fast enough? Contrary to what Mr. Ahmadi says, *Ghazna* wasn't nearly as busy as *Cambridge Kabobs*. Maybe they're struggling financially and she was the price they paid."

"But then you'd be looking at the Afghan equivalent to organized crime," Mike said. "Does such a thing exist?"

"It does. Not to the same extent as the Italian Mafia or the Chinese Tongs, but there is some Afghan-based organized crime in the state, mostly around the heroin trade."

"But then the question really is—would your potential Afghan 'business man'—" Matt hooked air quotes around the word, "—be the person responsible for her death as well as her mutilation?"

"I don't have the answer to that yet. I.D. first, then motive. Hard to explain why she died until we know for sure who she was." Leigh drained her mug and glanced at her watch. "I'd better be on my way. I want to get this all typed up and filed so we can start fresh tomorrow. Thanks for the coffee."

"I'll walk you out." Matt waited while Leigh said goodbye to his father, and then followed her down the hall to the front foyer. "Make some time to stop by the lab tomorrow if you can. We'll have more for you by then. Aim for later in the day and hopefully Kiko will have a face for you as well."

"I'll find out what high school Hoor attended. Then, I'll try to get my hands on a yearbook."

"Sounds like a plan." He skimmed his fingertips down the outside of her arm. "I'm sorry you can't stay. I feel like we've been on the run for the past few days and haven't had a chance to catch up."

"Welcome to police work. You catch your spare moments when you can."

"I'll catch one now then." He moved in closer but then paused, his eyes half closed as he leaned into her on a slow inhale. "You smell . . . exotic."

She laughed and gave him a little push that didn't shift him even a fraction of an inch. "I probably smell like an Afghan restaurant. All those spices."

"It's making me hungry." But the glint in his eye betrayed his double meaning.

"Well, let's see if this will satisfy you for the time being until we can do better." Moving in, Leigh went up on tiptoe, slipping her fingers behind the nape of his neck to tip his head down to hers.

She caught her breath when he cupped her hips, pulling her in hard against him and meeting her mouth half way. This was still new for them; she was still learning his taste and the play of muscles shifting under her hands as he bent down to her. Sensitive to Mike down the hall, she reluctantly started to draw back, but he pulled her closer, sinking in to deepen the kiss, to luxuriate in it. Allowing herself a rare moment to throw caution to the wind, she acquiesced with a quiet sigh.

It was several minutes before he let her come up for air.

"Wow." She was more than a little breathless. "Now suddenly *I'm* hungry." But the clock was ticking on her drive back to Salem and she forced herself to step back. There was lots of time later to explore things further. To explore *him* further.

"You're sure you can't write your report here?" Tempting appeal shone in his eyes. "You're welcome to use my laptop."

"I'd love to, but there are a few other things I need to do back at the Unit." She turned to the door before she lost the battle with herself and stayed. "See you tomorrow."

At the bottom of the steps she turned, glancing back over her shoulder. Matt stood in the open doorway, one shoulder propped against the jamb, his arms crossed over his chest. He raised one hand in a silent farewell as she turned and strode toward her car.

CHAPTER SEVEN: DEVELOPER

Developer: a chemical solution which converts an invisible latent image on exposed film or photographic paper into a visible image.

Wednesday, 1:32 p.m.
Boston University, School of Medicine
Boston, Massachusetts

"Did I come too soon? Isn't she finished?" Leigh murmured under her breath to Matt as Kiko rifled through papers at her workstation.

"Just give her a minute. Kiko knows you want to understand what we do in the lab, and she wants to explain the process." He cast a sideways glance at the messenger bag she'd set on his desk. "Did you get it?"

"The yearbook? Yes." When he reached for it, she laid her own hand over the bag. "Let Kiko show me her reconstruction first. Then we'll see if it matches the photo."

Finally gathering her materials, Kiko crossed the floor toward them, Paul and Juka close behind. She set down a folder on the foot of the gurney that still held the victim's remains. "You're probably familiar with the most common type of facial reconstruction—the three-dimensional kind using plasticine over the skull?"

"Yes."

"What I've done is essentially the same thing, but in two dimensions instead of three."

"Is there a reason why you'd do it this way?"

"It takes less time and preserves the evidence. Come look." Kiko lead Leigh to the head of the table where the victim's skull was mounted on a low stand. The terrible gash was now filled in, the jagged pieces neatly glued back into place and small dots of varying thickness covered the face. "Tissue depth markers have to be applied no matter what type of reconstruction you do." Kiko pointed to one of the flesh-colored cylinders protruding from the forehead. "Basically, there are charts we follow, based on pooled normalized data that tell us on average how thick the tissue of the face is in very precise locations. Tissue depth markers are applied over those landmarks. Now, if I was doing a full 3D reconstruction, I'd fill in the gaps between the markers with plasticine to give you a fleshed face. But it's a very time-consuming process and it completely covers the skull itself."

"So your process leaves the bone untouched except for these markers?"

"Right. So if we ever need to go back and examine the bone, it's not covered in plasticine. Not to mention this method can be done in a fraction of the time."

Leigh turned to Matt. "Is this something you normally do?"

Matt laughed. "Me? Never. I can't draw stick people. Usually a forensic artist does this kind of work, not an anthropologist. But we've got Kiko—who straddles the line between artist and scientist." He indicated the folder. "Walk Leigh through it."

Kiko pulled two 8"x10" photographs from the folder, laying them out on the gurney. The skull was depicted from both front and side, flanked by a ruler. "I've taken both front and side perspectives of the skull to use as the basis for the reconstruction."

"Why did you include the ruler?" Leigh asked. "Is that to ensure you get the photo back to life-sized?"

"Yes. The same charts that give us tissue depth also give details on soft tissue characteristics like the eyes, nose and lips, so it's crucial that when the photos are printed, they are exactly one-to-one in scale with the original skull. Once I had that, I overlaid the photos with a piece of transparent vellum and then sketched the face, based on both the actual bone structure and the normalized data. This is our victim." She removed two pieces of vellum from the folder, laying each of them exactly over its corresponding photo.

Leigh's breath froze in her lungs. Their victim had gone from colorless death to life-like Technicolor in a single moment. She reached out a hand and then abruptly pulled it back.

"Go ahead," Kiko encouraged.

Not willing to touch the images, Leigh leaned in, bracing her hands on either side of the remarkable artwork. Kiko had created a living, breathing girl from bare bone and bits of vinyl eraser. A girl she could recognize—and did.

The face that stared back at her was young and full of hope, and Leigh's heart squeezed at that life being cut short so early and so violently. Large, luminous brown eyes gazed out from over high cheekbones. Warm mocha skin stretched over the smooth forehead and narrow nose. She had a small mouth, but the full lower lip showed just the hint of a smile. A glimpse of brown hair showed at her crown and tumbled free of a dark green headscarf at her shoulders.

Leigh picked up the front-facing sketch to study it more closely, trying to examine the sketch with some of Matt's scientific objectivity—she wanted to make sure she was seeing what was really there, rather than what she wanted to see. "This is amazing." She met Kiko's gaze, saw the pride there. "Is this the first time you've done this?"

"Matt let me try it a couple of times with Old North remains. It's really just a hobby. I never thought it would come in handy . . . until now."

"You filled in details based on what we assume is her background? The hair, eyes and skin tone?"

"She did." Matt cut in before Kiko could answer. "But it's not an assumption anymore. I have the strontium data for you."

Leigh turned to stare at him in surprise. "Already?"

"I called in a favor and got the samples run on the mass spec this morning. From what we talked about last night, you need confirmation ASAP."

"I do. If what we suspect is correct, we might be looking at a flight risk."

"I wondered about that. You showing up at his restaurant must have set off all sorts of alarm bells. Okay, strontium in a nutshell so it makes sense for you. Strontium is a basic chemical element found in the soil and is incorporated into the plants that grow there. Herbivores, like cattle, eat those plants and incorporate that same strontium into their bodies. Humans eat those herbivores and incorporate it in turn. Now, there are four isotopes of strontium. Geographically, the relative ratios between each of those four isotopes at a location are constant and unique, like fingerprints. Depending on the characteristic ratios, we can tell where on the planet the strontium in the sample most likely originated. Follow?"

"I think so. The strontium in the soil eventually ends up in us." Leigh glanced over at the skeletal remains on the gurney. "And it must end up in the bones or this wouldn't be a useful exercise."

"A little gets into the soft tissue, but over ninety-five percent of it ends up as part of the skeleton. But it's how it ends up in the bone that's crucial. Strontium is like calcium—the content turns over approximately every six years, so reading the strontium content in the bones tells us where she lived for the last six years of her life." Matt carefully lifted the skull from the stand and tapped the front teeth with an index finger. "But, tooth enamel is formed during childhood and doesn't change over time. So strontium levels in the enamel tell us where she lived as a child."

Leigh had to force herself not to tap her foot impatiently when Matt took the time to painstakingly set the skull back on the stand before turning to face her. "And?"

"And we nailed it. She grew up in Central Asia, in an area including Afghanistan, but spent at least part of the last six years in the northeastern U.S."

"Part of the last six years? Can you tell how much?"

"Not exactly, but from the numbers, I'm thinking probably four or five years. The ratios aren't exactly the northeastern U.S. standard; they drift a bit from that, but not too much. That should give you a rough immigration window to confirm once you have a suspected ID." Matt paused for a moment, the set of his mouth telling her he was pushing discomfort aside in the interest of the case. "Kiko's got one other version of the sketches you need to see."

Leigh followed his pointed gaze back to Kiko who pulled another sheet of vellum from the folder. "Matt explained the implications of the bone damage to us. I thought you might find this useful."

Leigh accepted the page, seeing the vellum between her fingers but suddenly not able to feel it as horror washed over her, deadening her senses. The sketch depicted the same girl, but all hope and vitality had been wiped from her expression. Instead, distrust and fear filled the dark eyes above the gaping hole where her nose should have been. She glanced at Matt to find his gaze fixed on the sheet, his jaw clenched, fury glinting in his eyes.

"Whoever did this needs to pay." Paul nearly spat the words. "How could someone do such a thing?"

"You'd be amazed at what human beings do to each other," Juka said quietly. "Have you heard of Srebrenica?" At Paul's confused look, he frowned as if he'd been expecting that exact response. "Of course you haven't. Just some ugly history from back home in Bosnia."

Pictures flashed in Leigh's mind—aerial photographs of farms, twisted bodies in mass graves, rows of green draped coffins. "Very ugly, recent history," she agreed.

Surprise shone in Juka's eyes. Then he bowed his head to her in a respectful nod.

"Time to compare them." Matt went to his desk, returning with Leigh's bag.

"Compare what?" Kiko asked.

Leigh took the bag, forcing herself to tamp down on the certainty she felt so she didn't influence the others in any way. She flipped open the flap and pulled out a large, hardcover burgundy book. "I have a potential ID in mind—an Afghani girl who went to a Cambridge high school and who's been missing for about six months. Her parents say she went back to Afghanistan, but I have serious doubts." She held up the book. "This is the yearbook from her high school, her graduation year, so we can do a direct comparison to Kiko's sketch." She flipped the book open to the marked section and laid it flat on the end of the gurney.

The spread pages were crowded with color pictures of smiling faces, each graduate wearing a black robe with a burgundy and gold hood draped over their shoulders. The girls held roses while the boys held diplomas. Leigh scanned the pictures before tapping one. "Here she is. Hoor Ahmadi." The girl in the photo was pretty, her face alight with happiness as she smiled at the camera. Leigh's stomach gave a single jump of acknowledgment and then settled in satisfaction.

She was certain now—they'd found her.

Bodies crowded as everyone leaned in, and if Leigh had any remaining doubts, they were quickly put to rest by the gasps and murmurs round her. A hand rested lightly at Leigh's hip just before Matt's words came near her right ear as he peered over her shoulder. "Well done, Kiko. It's an amazing likeness."

"Thanks." But there was no pride in Kiko's face or voice. Instead her gaze settled on the sketch of the mutilated girl. "But that's the real picture. The real girl."

"I'm afraid so," Leigh said. "But try not to dwell on that. You've done incredibly good work and it's given me what I need to get my warrants. Now the real investigation can begin."

"I think we're looking at part of the investigation right here," Matt said.

Leigh glanced back at him. "What do you mean?"

"Look at her. She looks like a typical teen. No headscarf, her hair down, wearing makeup; it's not heavy but it's there. She's showing her beauty to the world. Exactly what her father would despise."

"She looks Western," Paul said. "Kind of exotic with her coloring, but Western. You think that's what got her killed?"

Matt stepped back. "A man like her father would consider this kind of disobedience a disgrace to his name and to the family. He might retaliate, especially in a way that marred that beauty forever."

"But mutilating her and killing her are two different events that happened months apart," Juka stated. "Doing the one doesn't necessarily make you guilty of the other."

"It's a valid point," Leigh agreed.

"Flaunting her beauty in a graduation photo would be pretty daring," said Kiko. "It's one thing to put a little makeup on at school where your parents won't see you—lots of girls do—but having a photo taken like that would be risky. It's a permanent record of your disobedience."

"Maybe her parents never saw the photo," Juka suggested. "She's the eldest child of parents raised outside of America. They might not even realize that such a photo would ever be taken, and she likely never brought it home. Perhaps this is the only copy of it. But it may have been a true record of who she was, at least at school."

"Exactly what I'm going to find out," Leigh said. "I have time to get back to the school. I'll see if I can find a teacher who knew her during her last year." Leigh closed the yearbook, and then stacked the photos and sketches, purposely keeping the intact, hopeful face on top. "It's remarkable work, Kiko. You've given her back her face and her name."

"Good work, guys," Matt said. "You've had a long morning. Go take a break and grab some lunch."

In under a minute the lab was empty and quiet. "That was fast," Leigh said.

"Grad students can always eat." Matt leaned against the corner of his desk. "When will you get your warrants?"

"I'll start the process as soon as I get back to Salem later this afternoon. I should have them in hand at some point tomorrow." Leigh ran her fingertips lightly over the page, feeling the soft impressions of the pencil lines under her touch. She took in the details again, marveling at the skill that brought bone to life. "She was really beautiful. Even without makeup and with her hair covered."

"She was. And for men from that area of the world, such beauty would be considered dangerous."

Leigh's fingers froze against the paper as her gaze darted upwards. "How?"

"It's all part and parcel of the chadri. A woman is to remain covered, hidden from the eyes of all but her husband and immediate family."

"Because to show off her beauty would invite a man's attention? Because men are too weak to be able to resist?"

"Something like that. Before the Taliban took power in Afghanistan, women didn't wear the full chadri as a rule. But the Taliban required it at all times. Its use declined a decade ago, but lately it's been increasing again."

"The women I met in the restaurants yesterday mostly wore head scarves, but their faces were uncovered."

"Considering the events of 9/11, Americans might not respect the chadri the same way that those back at home would." When Leigh started to protest he held up a hand to stop her. "I know and I agree. Just because they come from that part of the world, doesn't make them responsible for the terrorist attacks, but tell that to the general population here. Sometimes people act first and ask questions later. If this girl had to wear a chadri at all times, some might have not taken to it too kindly. And if we can't link her mutilation and death, then that could bring us back to the bikers in Lawrence and their dislike of immigrants."

"I'm not writing them off completely, but I think planting that ribbon on the body was pure misdirection, especially after yesterday. I wasn't getting the full story from her family, so we'll just have to uncover it ourselves." She tipped the drawing toward him. "This will go a long way toward that."

For a moment they both stared at the sketch. Their victim now had a face and a name.

It was a huge step forward.

CHAPTER EIGHT: PAINTING WITH LIGHT

Painting With Light: a technique for creating long-exposure photographs. A camera is mounted on a tripod and placed in a darkened room with the shutter left open. The photographer uses various types of lights to cast interesting patterns onto the subject.

Wednesday, 3:25 p.m.
Oliver Wendell Holmes High School
Cambridge, Massachusetts

"You're sure it's Hoor?" The young woman absently stroked a hand over her distended stomach, as if to take comfort from the child within.

"As sure as we can be until DNA is confirmed." Mouth dry, Leigh eyed the woman intently. The young teacher sitting across from her looked as if she might go into labor at a moment's notice. Leigh had heard stories from colleagues about delivering babies in unlikely places, but she had no desire to experience such a situation herself. "Are you sure you're up to this, Mrs. Wilson?"

Mrs. Wilson tried to smile, but it was lopsided. "Don't worry, I have more than a month to go. He's stubborn and not ready to budge yet." She sighed heavily, sorrow layering the sound. "I want to do what I can to help."

"If you wouldn't mind looking at the artist's sketch of the victim? To confirm?"

"Of course."

Leigh pulled Kiko's front-facing sketch of the smiling girl from the folder on her lap.

Mrs. Wilson's breath caught and her eyes filled as she took the outstretched sketch. "Oh honey, what happened to you?" She looked up a Leigh, blinking back tears. "That's Hoor Ahmadi. I haven't seen her in over a year, but she's unmistakable."

"You taught her English during her final year?"

"Yes. She was a good student and a kind friend."

"It sounds like you knew her fairly well."

"Better than most of my students. We had class at the end of the day, and Hoor would sometimes linger after the other students left. She talked about going to college and getting her Bachelor of Education. She wanted to teach, girls especially. She mentioned on several occasions the idea of going abroad to teach English as a second language to girls in her own country." She frowned. "From what she told me, many girls don't have the opportunity to be educated in Afghanistan."

"She's right, many don't. It was an admirable goal."

"But an unreachable one for her, I suspect." Mrs. Wilson handed the sketch back to Leigh.

"Why do you say that?"

The younger woman winced suddenly and then held up a hand as Leigh half rose from her chair in alarm. "It's all right. He's going to be a soccer star if the way he kicks now is any indication." She tried to find a comfortable position in the wooden desk chair, but her twisted expression and heavy sigh made it clear she wasn't successful. "I don't think her parents approved of her plans for an education. They seemed very . . . conservative."

"Conservative?"

"I remember the one and only time I met Hoor's parents. We were studying the essay *A Room of One's Own* by Virginia Woolf in class. It seems Mr. Ahmadi found the book in Hoor's bedroom and objected to his daughter reading 'feminist filth' as he described it."

"But it's part of the curriculum?"

"It is. By today's standards, Ms. Woolf's views about a woman's freedoms are not considered earth-shattering—at least not to North Americans. But Mr. Ahmadi vehemently objected to it. The curious thing is the Ahmadis made an appointment to come see me to discuss the issue, but when I met with them one day after school, Hoor was dressed in a way I'd never seen before—she was covered from head to toe. Mr. Ahmadi was wearing a small cap, but his wife and daughter were both wearing a covering from the top of their head to their knees."

"A chadri. Complete with netting over the face?"

"Yes. I didn't even know which woman was my student until her mother finally said something. But Mr. Ahmadi did most of the talking." Her fingers twisted together and her forehead wrinkled with concern. "That wasn't Hoor at all. Normally she was a very animated young woman, but the girl under the veil was another person. However, the next day, she was back to being herself and never said a word about it. But she seemed relieved when I assigned her a different book to read."

"When she normally came to school, she wasn't covered like that?"

"Not at all. She looked like any other normal student. She was considered a bit conservative for a teen, and her clothes weren't designer label, but she didn't seem to care about that."

"Did she wear a headscarf?"

"Never. She had beautiful hair and she usually wore it quite simply."

"Did you ever see her come to school covered up, only to take on a Western appearance once she got here?"

"Except for that one time, she always dressed like one of our typical kids. Assuming she had to leave the house covered like that, she must have been dressed normally underneath and had a place outside of school—maybe a public washroom or a friend's house—where she removed her robes and head covering."

"Did she wear makeup?"

Mrs. Wilson froze momentarily, her narrowed gaze locked unseeingly on a point over Leigh's shoulder. "It was subtle, but she did use a little makeup to highlight her looks."

"Did the boys go after her?" Leigh asked.

"They tried, but she always rebuffed them. She was friendly with them, but in a standoffish kind of way. She had her eye on the ball when it came to school. She felt she was lucky to live somewhere where education was so accessible and wanted more of it." A shout came from outside the classroom's open door, drawing their attention, and two boys in high top sneakers and basketball uniforms sprinted by. Their footsteps slowly faded into the distance.

"She was raised in Afghanistan, so she'd understand the value of American female independence," Leigh said. *She'd likely understand it just from living under her father's roof.*

"And now she's gone." Mrs. Wilson's shoulders sagged, her body curling as far forward as her belly would allow. "Why does it always seem like we lose the good ones? She had so much promise and such dreams. She could have made a difference. Some kids walk through my door and I know there's nothing I can do for them; their path is already set. But students like Hoor, that's where we can make a real difference. Pay it forward, so to speak, and then watch those kids pick up our torch. She had such light, and now it's extinguished."

Leigh leaned forward, laying her hand over the other woman's. In the silence that passed between them, Leigh knew the other woman understood her tacit promise: there would be justice for Hoor.

CHAPTER NINE: FIXER

Fixer: a chemical solution that converts light-sensitive silver halides into grains of silver that cannot be changed by further exposure to light. Without fixer, the developed image will darken and vanish if exposed to light.

Thursday, 4:48 p.m.
Ghazna Restaurant
Cambridge, Massachusetts

Even though it was nearly the dinner hour, the kitchen of *Ghazna* was eerily quiet—no pots clanging, knives thumping on cutting boards, china clattering, or orders barked from the head chef. Instead, the cooks and wait staff stood in a tight knot in one corner of the dining room, whispering and glancing suspiciously at Leigh. Tariq Ahmadi stood with his wife and son near the bar, his furious gaze locked on her unblinkingly.

Matt and Leigh stood by the front door, watching as the techs from Crime Scene Services moved systematically through the restaurant. Every once in a while the kitchen door would swing open and Leigh could see the techs at work before the door swung shut again.

"We didn't find a damned thing at the house," Matt murmured. "I thought we had something when we found that locked room down in the basement . . . until it turned out to be nothing but old business records. What if you don't find anything here either?"

Leigh struggled to tamp down the frustration building inside her at Matt's question, reminding herself he was only giving voice to her own concerns. "I told you this is what could happen. But you wanted to come anyway."

"I was hoping you'd be wrong."

"He had a full forty-eight hours on us. If Hoor's belongings were still at the house on Tuesday, there was plenty of time to get rid of them. But I bet her things were gone long before this. He couldn't afford to be found with them. He probably also didn't want a physical reminder of his failure to control his daughter."

When Matt and Leigh had arrived at the Ahmadi house that morning at just past eleven o'clock, they had a search warrant in hand and a Crime Scene Services team in tow. Mrs. Ahmadi was alone, but her husband had stormed through the front door within minutes of his wife's frantic call. Incensed at the intrusion, he'd done his best to block the search already in progress until the threat of arrest finally convinced him to step back. The search continued for several hours, but no sign of the girl had come to light. Her room was neatly organized, but the dresser drawers were empty, and no toiletries crowded the bathroom. When Leigh questioned how clean the room was, Tariq told them his wife cleaned regularly; there was no excuse for a dirty or dusty house. When Hoor came home, she could return her belongings to their proper place and pick up her life in Cambridge as if she'd never left.

Standing outside the two-story clapboard duplex, Leigh had received the crime scene report she expected but desperately didn't want—there was no sign of the girl inside, from clothing, to the simplest of beauty products, to fingerprints in her ruthlessly clean room. Leigh's best hope was several lengths of pipe found in the basement that were taken into evidence to sample for remnants of blood and DNA. Then the team had moved on to the next part of the search warrant—the restaurant.

Matt's words broke into her thoughts. "Another day or two and he wouldn't have had to worry. Remember, the trash at that landfill was earmarked for incineration. There wouldn't have been any proof of the girl's death. It's hard to pin a murder on someone when there's no body." His gaze remained fixed flatly on Tariq, as if daring him to step out of line. "The call to the tip line—that's when it all went wrong for him. There's no other information on who reported the body?"

"Nothing. I've been thinking about that too. It was a girl. Maybe it was one of Hoor's friends?"

"But how would a friend know that kind of information? And even if a friend thought Hoor had been killed, how could she know where the body was dumped?"

"I know, it doesn't work for me either. Especially since Hoor was locked away for six months while everyone was told she went back home to Afghanistan. No one else would question it the way we do, they'd just accept it."

Matt stepped a little closer, angling his head closer to hers as he kept his voice low. "I've been going over something in my head."

"What?"

"Her room looked clean. Maybe too clean."

"I thought the same thing. Not just cleaned but sanitized. But if they're sticking to their story that Hoor left six months ago, it's not unreasonable we wouldn't find much trace of her after all this time."

"Convenient," Matt commented. "I didn't pick up on it then, but I realize now what it is about the room that bothers me."

"What?"

"Did you notice the—"

"Are you done now, Trooper Abbott?" Tariq's raised voice from across the room cut through Matt's words. "I think I've been more than patient as you've violated my family's privacy. But now you're intruding into my dinner hour and hurting my business."

Leigh laid a hand on Matt's arm, silently telling him to wait there for her, and crossed the room. "I'll let you know when we're done, Mr. Ahmadi. These things can't be rushed. We might miss something."

Tariq put an arm around his son, pulling the boy against him, unconcerned when the boy stiffened at the contact. "Then let my family go. You're scaring them."

"I'm afraid not, Mr. Ahmadi." But Leigh bent down, bracing her hands on her knees so she could look the boy in the eye. "What's your name?"

The boy pulled away from his father, moving closer to his mother. "Saleeh." The boy's voice was high-pitched, and given his slender frame, it was clear puberty was still years off.

"Do you understand we're worried about your sister?"

Tariq grabbed Leigh's arm firmly, jerking her upright. "I told you she left the country."

Leigh knocked the offending hand away easily. "I suggest you keep your hands off me," she snapped. "It would be my pleasure to arrest you for assaulting an officer." She stared at him coldly. "Hoor came to Massachusetts on an Afghan visa. If she left, she'd have had to show her green card. There's no record of that. Your daughter never left this country." She stepped up to him, a smile pulling at the edges of her lips as fury distorted his expression. "So what happened to her?"

"I can prove to you she's there. I can call her and you can talk to her."

"You could have someone stand in for her. Only an exact DNA match will satisfy me at this point. And speaking of which . . ." She bent down to the boy again. "Saleeh, we're going to take a DNA sample from both you and your parents."

"What?" Tariq practically shouted the word. "You will do no such—"

Leigh rounded on him so quickly he took an involuntary step backwards, his gaze darting to the hand she instinctively laid over her sidearm. "It's in the search warrant, Mr. Ahmadi. If I need to call in more officers to hold you down while I take the sample, I will do it."

"Will it hurt?" The small voice drew her attention.

With effort, Leigh gentled her voice, fighting past the anger. "No." She turned and pointed at Matt across the room. "Do you see that man? That's Dr. Lowell. He's going to run a cotton swab over the inside of your cheek." She left unmentioned that Matt was a Ph.D., not a medical doctor; it was a detail the boy didn't need. "It won't hurt at all."

"Okay."

"I'll need swabs from both of you as well," Leigh said to the Ahmadis. "Once that's done and the search is complete, assuming we don't find anything, we'll turn the site back over to you and you can open for business."

She crossed the room back to Matt. "We'll do swabs in a few minutes."

"Sure."

"Now, what were you saying about Hoor's room?"

"You said yourself it was very clean. But did you notice the fresh paint?"

Something was playing at the back of Leigh's mind, something she couldn't quite put her finger on. But Matt's question caught her, causing her to look up at him sharply. "No, I missed that. The whole room?"

"No. What I noticed was the door. It's either new or newly repaired and painted."

"Repaired? Why?"

"I wonder if there was an outside lock on that door before and they had to cover up the fact someone was held prisoner there."

"If that's true, then they would have had to repair the jamb too."

"I think the window was also painted shut. That didn't strike me as being new, but it would mean she couldn't get out that way, if she wanted to escape."

"I'll go back and check the pictures the techs took for confirmation. Nice catch."

"Thanks."

"I think the techs are nearly done. We can start swabbing with the boy and move on to—"

And just like that, the prickling little thought clarified and she gasped in surprise, spinning around to face the far end of the room.

Matt caught her arm. "What? What's wrong?"

"That voice."

"What voice?" Frustration built in Matt's tone. "Leigh, what are you talking about?"

Leigh scanned the group across the room, her gaze finally coming to rest on the boy standing with his mother as the pieces fell into place. "The tip line call. It wasn't a girl who called—it was a pre-pubescent boy. It was the brother. And if that's true, and he knew about the body dump, then his connection to it limits who could be responsible."

"You're thinking it points straight to Tariq?"

"It feels right to me. And did you notice how when his father touched him, Saleeh stiffened? He's scared of him."

"I bet the man is hell on wheels as a father. We think he beat his daughter, so beating his son isn't much of a stretch. And the boy would be even more scared if he knew the man had committed murder. If that's true, then the kid's got serious guts if he reported his father."

A loud crash echoed from the kitchen. Tariq loosed a string of angry words in a foreign tongue and bolted for the swinging door. As he disappeared into the back, several voices raised in argument.

"Let's find out for sure," Leigh said. "It's never going to be safer for the boy than when his father's out of the room. His mother's here, so he's not without a parental guardian."

They crossed back to mother and child, Leigh's attention fixed on the boy who stared back at her with a combination of fear and hope. For the first time in the case, Leigh felt their answer was within reach, but she was careful to keep triumph from her voice and expression. "Saleeh, can I ask you a few questions?"

The boy's nervous gaze flicked momentarily to his mother, who remained silent, and he nodded.

"It was you who called the tip line last Thursday to report your sister's body at the dump, wasn't it?"

Frozen, Saleeh simply stared at her, eyes huge, panic flickering in their depths. His gaze darted from Leigh, to the kitchen door, and back again.

Leigh crouched down in front of him, purposely making herself small and less threatening, but she knew she wasn't who the boy feared. "You haven't done anything wrong. You're not in trouble. In fact, whoever called did right by your sister. We might have lost her otherwise, but now we've found her and she can be buried properly, as she should be. Do you miss your sister?"

He folded his lips together, but gave one sharp nod of his head.

"Do you know what happened to her?"

"Saleeh, don't answer that." Tariq suddenly stepped between them, forcing his son back a pace and nearly knocking Leigh to the carpet. He had come back into the restaurant while her attention was fixed on his son. "Trooper, you may not talk to him without our lawyer present."

Leigh pushed off the floor, fixing him with a level stare. "I'm happy to wait for your lawyer."

"I will go call him." He waved a finger between his wife and son. "Say nothing until I return." Tariq turned and marched to his office on the far side of the bar. The door closed behind him with a sharp snap.

Matt moved up quickly behind her. "I really don't like the idea of him in another room by himself."

"Me either." She went to the door, trying the handle. "It's locked." She pounded on the door. "Mr. Ahmadi! Mr. Ahmadi, open up."

A crash from inside the room was the only answer.

Leigh whirled on the other woman. "Is there another way out of that room?"

Wide-eyed, Mrs. Ahmadi shook her head frantically. "Just a window to the alley."

"Damn it, he's making a run for it!" Leigh sprinted for the front door, Matt only steps behind. They pushed through the door, pounding along the sidewalk, rounding the corner of the building just in time to see a dark form dart out of sight at the end of the alley. "He went that way." She tore down the alley, past a window, its glass shattered, and a mangled wooden chair crumpled against the opposite alley wall.

They careened around the corner, partially skidding on loose gravel underfoot. Matt reached out a hand to steady himself on the corner of the building as he took the curve. Ahead of them, Tariq had a fifty foot lead and was sprinting away as fast as he could.

They gave chase, slowly gaining on him over two blocks. Matt let out a strangled curse when Tariq turned left down another alley, disappearing from view. Seconds later they took the same turn, but the alley was deserted. Coming to a four-way cross flanked by the featureless backs of local businesses, Leigh stopped, panting, looking in every direction.

"I don't see him," she huffed. "Which way did he go?"

"No idea." Matt's words came out on a gasp for breath. "You pick a direction and I'll take another. He'll get away for sure if we take this to committee."

Leigh threw him an irritated glance, but took off at a run, picking the alley to her right as Matt chose the passage straight ahead. Making another turn to her left, Leigh found herself in a short, dead-end passageway lined with overfilled dumpsters. Cursing, she turned back, retracing her steps and picking a different alley. Another turn took her back toward the main street that ran along the Charles River. Breaking out from between two buildings into the late afternoon sun, she spotted Matt half a block up the street. He stood, hands on hips, scanning for any sight of Tariq.

Panting and gasping for breath, Leigh turned around desperately, searching for any sign of their suspect. Across from them, through a scattering of trees laced with gold and scarlet, lay the Charles River. It was dotted with sail and motor boats—yacht club members taking advantage of the last of autumn's temperate weather.

"There." Matt's shout had her already in motion toward him before she could spot anything specific. "He's going up those stairs." Matt ran after him, Leigh sprinting to catch up. A block ahead, she spotted the dark figure of a man running up a long flight of concrete steps toward the Longfellow Bridge. A minute later, Matt reached the steps first. Breathing hard, Leigh pounded up after him.

Tariq was a quarter of the way across the span as they sprinted down the sidewalk after him, weaving around pedestrians. He knocked over an elderly man, sending him sprawling into the street amidst a chorus of car horns and screeching tires.

Matt darted out into traffic, hauling the man up off the road and onto the sidewalk. He waved Leigh on. "Keep going."

Leigh continued the chase, knowing Matt would follow as soon as he could.

The gap between herself and Tariq was closing rapidly as his stamina started to flag. He staggered, nearly falling, and only his wildly flailing arms kept him upright. Righting himself, he suddenly veered left, cutting along the sidewalk that curved around one of the central towers that gave the landmark its colloquial name—the 'Salt and Pepper Shaker Bridge'. He disappeared around the far side of the tower.

Leigh took the curve around the tower at a flat-out sprint, nearly throwing herself against the encircling stone wall in an attempt to stop abruptly on the far side at the sight of her suspect. Her service revolver was immediately in hand, the barrel steady on Tariq's chest, her fingers clenched tight on the grip to hold it still when her hand threatened to shake. "Don't move."

Then she realized he wasn't standing at the short wall, but *behind* it. He'd climbed over and only his white knuckled grip on the lip kept him from tumbling into the Charles River forty feet below. "Mr. Ahmadi, I want you to climb back over the wall." She'd been on this bridge before, leaning over the edge of the stone parapet to look down into the choppy, windswept waters below. She knew he was perched on his toes on a stone lip mere inches wide. One false move could mean death.

"Why? So you can arrest me and throw me in your American jail?"

"You killed your daughter." Her heart was starting to slow, and the heavy thump of its pounding in her ears starting to fade. "And then tried to cover your tracks just in case she was ever discovered by pointing fingers at the Merrimac Arms' bikers. How did you get that ribbon? You wouldn't have been welcome at that bar."

"An honest working man wouldn't be welcome among those horrible men," he spit out. "An out of town visitor stopped at my restaurant after the last race and left that ribbon behind on the floor. It did exactly what I intended if you thought one of them was guilty."

"We explored the possibility, but the mutilation pointed too strongly at someone from Hoor's own country for us to be distracted for long."

"She deserved it. She was supposed to be named for the virgin maiden of paradise. Instead, she took on the American meaning. She was a whore."

"Because she didn't cover herself from head to toe? Because she dared to show her beauty to the world?" Pounding footsteps heralded Matt's arrival and Leigh held out her left arm, slowing him when inertia pushed him toward the edge. "You had a smart, kind, beautiful daughter. You mutilated her for that?"

"She dishonored her family. She never did so again."

"She never had the chance. You kept her prisoner in her own house."

Tariq spat at her feet. "She was no longer my daughter. I remember my daughter fondly. I have no idea who that creature was. She was a disgrace. Worse, she tainted her brother. He was a good boy, but because of her influence, he started to stray from the old ways."

"He was growing up in America. You brought him here; what did you expect?"

"I expected him to do as he was told. Instead, he disobeyed me and lied to me on several occasions. And in the end, he betrayed me. That was also her doing."

Leigh shook her head in disgust. "Always the woman's fault, isn't it?"

"It would not be if she did as she was told. A woman should obey her father, brothers, and husband. She needs a man's guiding hand."

"Don't you mean 'fist'? Your daughter's body showed signs of abuse—a broken arm and indications of a blow from a fist to the face."

"She was stubborn. She needed to learn respect. It is the way of the world."

"Not my world. What did Hoor do that caused you to beat her to death? We know she was beaten and killed by a blow to the head with a pipe."

"She tried to escape. She even made it outside the house, but I caught her before she made it onto the street."

"You just wanted to save your own ass. No decent person with a backbone would stand for what happened to her. You would have paid for what you'd done to her if she'd been seen by anyone in the outside world. You couldn't allow that to happen."

"Leigh, let me past," Matt said. "I'll pull him back over."

She shook her head stubbornly. "No way. Too dangerous. He could yank you over the edge."

"I can handle him," Matt scoffed.

He started to move forward and she slapped her hand against his chest, feeling muscles made strong by rowing, but ignoring the strength they implied. "Stay back. I'm not risking your life. Mr. Ahmadi, I need you to climb back over the wall."

"I would rather die a free man than disgraced in your jail."

She saw the intent in his eyes even before he moved, and ignoring her own instructions to Matt, lunged for him. But it was already too late. He pushed off the railing, his body arcing in mid-air before dropping from sight.

Jamming her gun back in the holster, Leigh raced for the edge just in time to see his sprawled body hit the water. Then . . . nothing.

A flurry of activity beside her drew her attention and dread washed over her as she turned to see Matt kicking off his shoes. "What are you doing?"

"Going after him."

"Are you *insane?*" Her hand clamped down over his arm. "That's at least forty feet. The drop could kill you. And if it doesn't, the river will finish the job."

"I'm an experienced swimmer and I know this river like the back of my hand." He leaned over and looked again. No sign of anyone in the water. "Leigh, there's no time to discuss this." Matt pulled from her grasp and swung his legs over the ledge. Then with one last look over his shoulder, he jumped into the void.

"NO!" Her heart in her mouth, she watched his body slice through the air, cleanly cutting the water below, the waves closing over his head.

Then there was nothing but the waves and the wind whistling mournfully around the tower.

CHAPTER TEN: LATENT IMAGE

Latent Image: an invisible picture which cannot be seen by the human eye until the photosensitive material containing it has been developed.

Thursday, 5:21 p.m.
The Charles River
Cambridge, Massachusetts

The dual shock of cold river water coupled with the force of hitting the surface took Matt's breath away, leaving him disoriented and struggling to stay focused. Sinking fast, his body spun helplessly, tossed by his own momentum and the river's current where it eddied around the bridge abutment. Opening his eyes, all Matt saw was tumbling dark water without a glimpse of sunlight to show him the way to the surface. Somersaulting through the murky gloom, the pressure built steadily in his head and chest. The temptation to ease the pressure by releasing some of his precious air grew with each passing second.

Matt fought against the panic building alongside the ringing in his ears. If he gave in, he'd drown.

Moments flashed through his mind.

Standing with his mother at the base, dressed in fatigues, his duffel at his feet. Her hand running over his freshly buzzed hair before she pulled him close. Her voice a whisper in his ear: I love you. I'm so proud of you.

Again in fatigues, sitting at his father's bed, grieving both the loss of his mother and the broken wreck of this once vital man.

The hopeful faces of his students as they entered his lab for the very first time. Later, the shock and horror as they gazed down at Tracy Kingston, their first murder victim, spread before them in the clearing.

Leigh stretched under him across his bed, her hair a pale

shimmer over the dark quilt as she reached for him.

Clarity and focus slammed back into place.

Leigh. The case.

Tariq.

With effort, Matt pushed it all away, telling himself to ignore the panic even as his lungs burned and his head started to swim. Forcing his body to stillness, he allowed logical thought to cut through the panic. Spreading out his arms and legs, he let the buoyancy of his own lungs show him the way up. For a moment, nothing happened and the panic that lapped hard at the edges of his consciousness threatened to swamp him.

Then he felt it. It was slight, but the pressure against his ribcage started to ease. Relief flooded through him; he was rising through the water.

His head broke the surface and he gasped, glorious fresh air filling his oxygen-starved lungs. Pushing his wet hair out of his eyes, he looked up to the tower where Leigh still leaned over the edge, frantically searching for him. Her body sagged against the wall for just a moment in relief and then she was gone, and he could just see her head and shoulders as she sprinted down the bridge, back the way they'd come.

Matt spun in the water, searching over the choppy surface for any sign of Tariq. In the distance, he could see boats headed directly for him. Onlookers must have seen one or both of them going off the bridge and were coming to help. One of the boaters stood at the bow, waving both arms at him. Thrusting one hand from the water, Matt waved back.

He never saw the blow coming.

Tariq came out of the water, leading with a fist that caught Matt just under his right eye. The force of the blow pushed him back underwater, and, unprepared for the sudden dunking, gritty water flowed into his mouth and down his throat. Struggling back toward the light, Matt broke the surface, coughing and choking.

Tariq was right on top of him again, pushing him back under. Matt had just enough time for a quick gasp of air before he was submerged again. Pulling his legs up, he rammed his heels into

Tariq's stomach, hearing the grunt of pain even underwater. He shot to the surface, using the momentum from pushing off Tariq to gain precious inches. The roar was building in the distance; glancing over his shoulder Matt could see three motor boats speeding toward them at full throttle.

Time to end this now.

"It's over, Tariq. Help is coming. You can't get away."

"Maybe I am not trying to get away. Maybe I am going to drown and want to take you with me."

Tariq threw both arms around Matt, holding on with the strength of desperation as they both sank like stones. Matt struggled hard against his hold, feeling his grip loosen slightly. Pulling his arms in tight against his body, he clenched his fists as if he was sitting at the oars and pulled back sharply in a rowing stroke, cleanly breaking Tariq's hold and allowing him to swim clear once more.

Matt broke the surface first, knowing his best chance to beat the other man was to catch him in the brief second when he surfaced, blinded by water and the setting sun. Treading water, he waited, his patience straining tighter and tighter with each passing second.

Where the hell was he?

Then a head broke the water three feet away, facing away from him. Matt moved quickly, shooting forward to come within reach of the other man. Tariq turned only when Matt was practically on top of him. Matt pulled back, putting all the anger and loathing he felt for this man behind his fist, and directed a devastating punch at his nose. There was a sickening crunch of bone as Tariq bellowed in pain and went under the waves. Matt grabbed a handful of collar, heaving him back up, while simultaneously sliding his free arm around Tariq's throat and tightening until the other man stopped struggling.

"Don't move," Matt snarled in Tariq's ear, "or I'll cut off your air and let the guys in the boat haul you aboard unconscious." He tightened his hold ever so slightly until Tariq stopped fighting.

Struggling with the extra load, Matt dragged them both further into open water and toward the approaching boats. When a large motor boat finally pulled up beside them, two men stood on the stern swim platform. They dragged Tariq on board, and then returned to help Matt. He quickly explained the situation, pointing back toward shore and the dock of a nearby marina where a Cambridge police car was just pulling up, siren wailing and lights flashing.

Matt collapsed back on a bench, his heart rate slowing as he was able to get enough air into his lungs. Adrenaline started to drain out of his system, leaving his limbs feeling leaden and ungainly. Tariq sat in a dripping heap in a corner of the boat, one of their rescuers standing over him threateningly with the sharp end of a gaff hook pointed at his chest.

The boat lurched as the pilot pulled back on the throttle, sending them speeding back toward land to meet the incoming officers.

***

Thursday, 5:43 p.m.
The Charles River
Cambridge, Massachusetts

The thump of boots down the dock drew Matt's attention from the Cambridge police officer questioning him.

Leigh slowed from a jog down to a fast walk as she approached the men. She flashed her badge at the uniformed officer. "Trooper Abbott out of Essex. Dr. Lowell is with me."

"So he says." He held out a hand to her. "Officer Perkins, CPD. This is my partner Officer Donnelly. We responded to a 911 call about two men going off Longfellow Bridge. We held them both until we were relieved by a couple of guys from Field Troop H. They took one man into custody and asked us to wait here with this one until you arrived."

"The man in custody is my suspect. This is my partner. Thanks for helping us out."

"Our pleasure." The man gave her a brief nod and the two

officers strode off down the dock.

Leigh turned to Matt, who stood in a growing puddle of water, wrapped in a standard-issue gray police blanket. She looked him up and down, her shoulders relaxing fractionally when it was clear he was whole and unharmed. "I could kill you for pulling that stunt."

"Going off the bridge?" He smiled a little sheepishly. "Didn't really take the time to think that through."

"I guess not."

"Turned out okay though. I'm fine." He held out both arms, pulling the blanket wide. "Better than him anyway. I think I broke his nose when we were struggling in the water."

Stepping up to him, she ran gentle fingers under his right eye. "I see he gave almost as good as he got. You're going to have a hell of a shiner by tomorrow."

Matt grinned. "Paul's going to think I'm the coolest scientist on the planet."

Shaking her head at the idiocy of men, Leigh pulled the blanket more snugly around him. "The troopers are going to take Tariq over to Mass Gen for treatment, since it's just across the river. Then I'll take him in. Do you need to be looked at or would you just like me to drop you at home?"

He fixed her with a mock glare. "Like you even need to ask." Matt's hatred of hospitals and trauma treatment in general had become abundantly clear during their last case. "It's a bump, that's all. I'd rather go home and dry off."

"I thought that's what you'd say."

Leaving the dock, they trudged up the grassy hill to the state police car parked at the curb. As Leigh circled the hood to talk to the troopers through the open driver's window, Matt leaned down and looked at the stony-faced man sitting handcuffed in the backseat, staring straight ahead. Tariq was wrapped in an identical blanket, but the front of his was covered with trails of blood.

Matt couldn't contain a triumphant grin. *You're done, you bastard. Now you can't hurt anyone else.*

Leigh rapped her fist twice on the top of the car and stepped back as the troopers pulled away with their bloodied and battered passenger.

Starting down the sidewalk together, Matt caught her hand, lacing his fingers through hers. Her hand felt wonderfully warm against his river-chilled skin. "What do you think will happen to his wife and son?"

"Hard to say at this point. The argument could be made that she was an accessory or at least an accessory after the fact for both the killing and the mutilation. But any defense lawyer worth his salt could argue that she was in an abusive relationship and was terrorized into silence, possibly in an effort to protect her remaining child. At the very least, she'll be brought in for questioning. Then we'll see where the chips fall."

"And the son?"

"That one will depend heavily on the mother. If she's taken into custody, either a family member will need to step up or he'll have to go into the system. If Mrs. Ahmadi isn't taken into custody, then she and the boy will have to find a way to make it on their own." She swung their hands lazily between them and gazed out over the bobbing water of the Charles. "I have a feeling she's got an ally she's not aware of yet."

"Really? Who?"

"Farah Nazar from *Cambridge Kabobs*. She strikes me as someone who'd step forward at a time like this to help Mrs. Ahmadi." Leigh gave a pleased laugh. "Actually, I bet she'd relish the chance. Nothing would make her feel better than sticking it to Tariq by helping his wife run the family business. She'd consider that the ultimate payback. She really, *really* hates him and his archaic attitudes."

"I think I'd like to meet this Farah Nazar."

"I'm going to be tied up tonight with the case but how about dinner there tomorrow? I'm dying to try the food. It smelled amazing."

"That sounds like a great idea. So . . . another case down. You know, I think I'm beginning to like this work. It's surprisingly satisfying."

Leigh gave him a long sideways glance. "And to think you almost turned me down a few weeks ago. Just think of everything you'd be missing." The teasing tone melted away. "But seriously, without you and the students, I'm not sure we would have caught him. If you hadn't caught the marks from the mutilation or if Kiko hadn't been able to give her a face . . ."

"Or if you hadn't nailed the voice on the tip line." He gave her hand a squeeze. "Remember what Paul said after our first case about teamwork? That's the key with us. We each bring something unique to the investigation. It's all about the sum of the parts, not the individual players."

Leigh nodded. "It certainly shows in our results. I'm glad we can bring Hoor home. After the life she led, she deserves to finally rest in peace."

"With her name and face intact. And at least one of her family will want that too. Her brother literally took his life in his hands informing us about her body being in that garbage heap. I guess we don't know how he found out?"

"Not yet. I suspect he probably overheard a discussion between his parents and realized if he didn't move fast, it would be too late. And while I don't think he had anything to do with planting the ribbon on the victim, I need to confirm it. I'll call in a social worker from the Department of Children and Families to be present when we talk to him. A lot of the case could hinge on his testimony, so we need to cross every 'T'. But he's a gutsy kid."

"He's not *just* a kid; he's the man of the family now. And already a better man than his father ever was."

Hand in hand, they walked into the dusk of a late fall afternoon, another case closed and another victim returned to her family. They'd given a young girl back her identity when one of the people who should have loved her most had cruelly ripped it from her. They'd given her back her face, and the beauty she had the courage to show the world.

That's how she would be remembered.

ABOUT THE AUTHORS

A scientist specializing in infectious diseases, **JEN J. DANNA** works as part of a dynamic research group at a cutting-edge Canadian university. However, her true passion lies in indulging her love of the mysterious through her writing. Together with her partner **ANN VANDERLAAN**, a retired research scientist herself, they craft suspenseful crime fiction with a realistic scientific edge. Their Abbott and Lowell Forensic Mysteries include *DEAD, WITHOUT A STONE TO TELL IT*; NO ONE SEES ME 'TIL I FALL; *A FLAME IN THE WIND OF DEATH*; *TWO PARTS BLOODY MURDER;* and *LAMENT THE COMMON BONES*. As Sara Driscoll, they also write the FBI K-9s series, including *LONE WOLF, BEFORE IT'S TOO LATE*, and *STORM RISING*. The fourth book in the series, *NO MAN'S LAND*, will release in December 2019.

Ann lives near Murphy, North Carolina with four rescued pit bulls. Jen lives near Toronto, Ontario, with her husband, two daughters, and three rescued cats. You can reach her at *jenjdanna@gmail.com* or through her website at *https://www.jenjdanna.com*.

Made in the USA
Lexington, KY
26 August 2019